POLONAISE

Also by Anthony Bukoski

Twelve Below Zero
Children of Strangers

For Joue, Susan,
with Best Wishes,

POLONAISE

Stories by
ANTHONY BUKOSKI

Anthony Bukoski

SOUTHERN METHODIST UNIVERSITY PRESS
Dallas

These stories are works of fiction. Names, characters, places, and incidents are either the product of the author's imagination or are used fictitiously.

The stories in this collection first appeared in the following publications: "Pesthouse" in *New Orleans Review;* "Dry Spell" and "The Tools of Ignorance" in *Louisiana Literature: A Review of Literature and the Humanities,* Southeastern Louisiana University, Hammond, Louisiana; "The Absolution of Hedda Borski" as "The Spinster's Confession Regarding Her Sorrows" in *Twelve Below Zero* (New Rivers Press); "The Korporał's Polonaise" in *Wisconsin Fiction,* a special sesquicentennial issue of *Transactions of the Wisconsin Academy of Sciences, Arts and Letters,* Volume 85, 1997; "Bird of Passage" in *Short Story International* (International Cultural Exchange, Inc., Great Neck, New York); "Immigration and Naturalization" as "Lands Which May Be the Most Beautiful on Earth" in *Third Coast;* "Private Tomaszewski" as "Prisoner of War" in *Poet & Critic;* "The Wood of Such Trees" in *Alaska Quarterly Review;* "The Month That Brings Winter" as "The Dark Central Part of a Shadow" in *New Letters,* Volume 54, number 4, reprinted here with permission of *New Letters* and the Curators of the University of Missouri–Kansas City; and "A Concert of Minor Pieces" in *New Canadian Review.*

Requests for permission to reproduce material from this work should be sent to:
Rights and Permissions
Southern Methodist University Press
SMU Box 750415
Dallas, Texas 75275-0415

Cover art: Charles Burchfield, *Winter Twilight,* 1930. Oil on composition board. Sight: 27¾ x 30½ in. (70.5 x 77.5 cm.). Collection of Whitney Museum of American Art. Purchase. 31.128. Photograph copyright © 1998: Whitney Museum of American Art.

Cover design: Tom Dawson Graphic Design

LIBRARY OF CONGRESS CATALOGING-IN-PUBLICATION DATA

Polonaise : stories / by Anthony Bukoski. — 1st ed.
    p.   cm.
    Contents: Pesthouse — Dry spell — The absolution of Hedda Borski — The korporał's polonaise — The tools of ignorance — Bird of passage — The world at war — Immigration and naturalization — Private Tomaszewski — The wood of such trees — The month that brings winter, or, How Mr. Truzynski carried Vietnam home with him — A concert of minor pieces.
    ISBN 0-87074-434-8 (cloth : alk. paper)
    I. Title.
PS3552.U399P65   1999
813'.54—dc21   98-26101

Printed in the United States of America on acid-free paper

10 9 8 7 6 5 4 3 2 1

For *Dziaduś*, Helen, and Fran

I wish to express my deepest gratitude to Kathryn M. Lang, senior editor at Southern Methodist University Press, for believing in this book. I am also grateful to the novelist and short-story writer Shirley Ann Grau for her kindnesses to me over the years; to my teachers Thomas Napierkowski and George Gott for their abiding interest in this work; and to my friend John Hanson, the filmmaker, for his goodwill and encouragement. I am grateful as well to Michael Longrie and Barton Sutter for reading early versions of the manuscript and to the University of Wisconsin–Superior for its support.

CONTENTS

Pesthouse

1.

I'm not doing well, the doctors say; too much *okowita*, too much *wódka*. Still, I must record my thoughts. Down here at the college in Louisiana where my husband teaches my classes when I'm ill, I am a long way in time from the house where I was born. It's hot here, in the 90s and humid, whereas up north people are already shoveling snow and scraping ice.

Here is how the neighborhoods were in a childhood long ago. They still are this way, I should think. The Allouez section of Superior, Wisconsin, was Belgian, the north end French and Indian, and the gas plant neighborhood Slovak. Mine was Polish. It will stay Polish forever, nothing but Polish.

In 1945–46, the years I can't shake from memory, most of the neighborhood men returned from the war to work on the docks. Business at the markets and bakeries picked up, as it did in the taverns. Below the ham hocks at the the Parrot Tavern, I can remember a sign read:

WE FIX EVERYTHING BUT BROKEN HEARTS
AND THE CRACK OF DAWN.

Another, near the pigs' feet in the tavern below my family's flat, read:

> When you order a drink, you'll take what we give you
> and pay what we charge you . . . THANKS. CALL AGAIN.
> P.S. The above was only for the duration of the war.
> NOW THAT IT'S OVER, we will kiss your ass as usual
> at the WARSAW TAVERN.

St. Adalbert's, our parish church, was full at Mass in the postwar days when my father returned with the other GIs. It seems everyone was back but me. In the isolation hospital, The Pesthouse, which stood far back away in the fields past Eleventh Street, my skin was peeling. I was weak. A scarlet rash spread to my mouth. No one who hadn't had scarlet fever could enter the building. All night, children cried. In a ward below, an old man yelled *"zarażenie,"* which means "contagion, infection," then he'd yell something about Poland, as if my grandparents' country, having been overrun in 1939 and having suffered so much, was infected like me. Words I remember from the endless days of dreaming are "rash," "feverish," the *"zarażenie"* the old man hollered, and crazy things like "oxtail" or *"stoczek,* wax stand" that made no sense later. It was the time of disease. How many would contract polio, TB, scarlet fever? If my young brother Grzegorz handled something I touched at home, he'd have caught *skarlatyna.*

When we were young, my brother and I, there was never much sense to our lives. Here is an instance of senselessness: mother wasn't well with her respiratory problem, I was gone away to the isolation hospital, and Grzegorz was frightened of a man who—suitcases filled with uniforms and postcards of Morocco and Algeria—stepped off the train in Superior, Wisconsin. Our sickly father was home.

A week before, the Health Department had had to fumigate St. Adalbert's School or the infection—my own infection—would have spread. The Pesthouse, like the school, was also a sad place. Here were sickroom attendants, laundry workers with peeling hands, janitors who burned the dirty rags and bedclothes patients sweated through. Incinerators went day and night. You'd see the rags that pests and contagions inhabited lying on floors. "The causative agent usually enters the body through the nose or mouth . . . ," I've read about scarlet fever. No matter how clean The Pesthouse, there were places under the banister or where the linoleum curled that made you ill. Infections were forced out of the chimneys, wrapping the moon in smoky fingers. Not everything was burned up in the furnaces, though, as the place also caused a sickness of spirit that couldn't be treated.

Edda Wasko, a St. Adalbert's pupil, was on the third floor with me, though in the boys' wing. Whenever I saw him in the hall, he looked terrible with his rash-spotted neck, the dark lines beneath the eyes.

Seeing me one afternoon, which I keep thinking was the day after Father's return, he said, "Franny, look what someone gave me."

He held up a sheet of paper that must have been copied from the chaplain's book. The handwriting said:

> The regulation of sexual relations between husband and wife is a field of enormous influence of the priest. The priest must answer the questions of women whether conjugal onanism or using medicines after coitus is immoral, sinful, contrary to nature; whether certain kisses and touches are a sin and when . . .

After I read it, The Pesthouse grew quiet.

Probably my brother was happily sitting on Father's lap before the stove with the isinglass door when the nurse took the paper from me and, seeing what it was, insisted I have a Lysol bath. The palms and feet will peel for months after scarlet fever. All that morning in the winter light I'd been contentedly building pyramids of dead skin on the floor. Now the nurse who undressed me said, "Lie back in the water. Rest. I'll be in and out. Forget what you read." She peeled my skin before she left.

Sometimes delirious, sometimes clearheaded, I stared at the high ceiling, dreaming I was swimming in a warm, white sea until someone in my fever whispered, "You're peeling worse than ever."

Wiping the mirror by the door so he could see himself in it, Edda peeled a strip of skin from his shoulder. "Can I have some of yours?"

"Yes."

He liked watching me. He'd keep the skin, he said. He had a box for it.

Hearing the nurse, Mrs. Gustafson, he hurried out.

"Is there someone in the steam?" she asked.

"No one," I said.

"Let's check your fever," she said. "You must have terrible fevers."

"If they keep on, Mrs. Gustafson, will I peel to nothing?"

"What's more important is not whether you do, but whether you enjoy your baths."

"Yes, I do," I said.

"That's good. What's the little mound of stuff on the floor by your bed? Is that skin?"

"Yes."

"Well, we can't sweep it now. Your father's outside in the snow."

My father! I was so happy. Downstairs, he was calling up to the window in the girls' wing, "At home, Franciszka, we'll have a pretty time." The wind must've been blowing. He stumbled, caught himself—kept his arms out for balance. It was like he, too, was sick the way he paced back and forth, talking about how he loved autumn. It was windy. It must've been my fever that made him seem so odd. It wasn't autumn. It was January. It must've been our fevers.

"I'm sending a souvenir upstairs," he said. "Did you miss Papa?"

"Yes," I whispered.

"Come away from the window before you tire yourself, Franny," said Mrs. Gustafson.

"Does my *father* have scarlet fever?" I asked.

Outside the light snow was falling. I saw him wave a package, an envelope. I remember to this day that one corner of the envelope he sent to me read: "After 5 Days Return to: American South African Lines, Inc. New York 4, NY." Next to the words "US POSTAGE .03¢" in purple ink was a drawing of Uncle Sam in a top hat. Finger to his lips, he's saying, "Sh! Don't Discuss Troop Movements—Ship Sailings—War Equipment." My father'd brought to America wallet-sized photos and postcards, cloth insignias, letters from Mother. But here I'm rambling. Oh, I get off the point! They say drinking does it. I'll stay on course. I will. I promise myself this, if nothing more.

Here's what my father's souvenir postcards said: *"L'Algérie Ses Paysages Ses Types"*. . . *"Bonne Ouuée du Maroc."* I wonder why I have them with me when everything Father brought from the war should be in the teakwood box in the highboy upstairs, in the house in Superior where my brother lives; this is where we keep memories, in the childhood home. No matter now, I guess.

Here's a postcard: an Arab sitting cross-legged, sorting twine in a dirt passageway between buildings. Taken no doubt during the 1940s, it's called *"Kabyle fabricant de burnous."* It's no. 8000 of the *"Carte Postale"* series of M. Belkhir of 55, ch. de St. Roch, Nice. Here's another of a white-robed North African tapping a light drum he holds near his shoulder. No. 8021, it's called *"Négro jouant du Tamtam."* Here is a young girl on an ottoman. From her headdress, the lovely beadwork and light, thin metal ornaments fall to her naked breasts, which are accentuated as she poses with her arms behind her head. She wears wrist and ankle bracelets. The photographer has caught her smiling. He's told her, "Hold your breath. Breathe in, Bou-Saâda"; for you can see below her breasts the definition of the abdomen as she does. A shawl covers her knees. One naked leg rests on the ottoman's striped cover. No. 8032, *"Mauresque de Bou-Saâda dans son intérieur."*

A half-century ago, these cards entertained a feverish child. On one of them, my father wrote a few words to capture the feel of the native quarter of Old Medina. His words, coincidentally, describe The Pesthouse: "filth, stench, disease . . . high-pitched gibberish, scrawny hands and fingers." In those sickly days, I lay dreaming of the heat of that quarter in Old Medina, of the narrow passageways he'd haunted only a few months before. No shawl like Bou-Saâda's covered me when I showed my skin to Edda Wasko. In the days to come, I'd pray to Our Holy Mother. As the Polish nurses peeled me, they whispered as in an exorcism, *"dezinfekt . . . dezinfektować."* Scarlet fever hung in the steam. My temperature was 103. But ugly Franny survived.

It's so hard for me to think of those times. No one knew about my experiences in The Pesthouse. Has it been forty-eight years, fifty years? I've drunk through half of them to forget the person who's peeled away. After the cure I never looked at The Pesthouse for a long time. I didn't look at the wanderer Casimir either.

2.

My father was a husky man, loud, husky, disoriented. Born August 1908, he died in December 1967. I repeat this: "My father's name was Casimir Stasiak."

In 1945 his brown hair rose stiffly from the forehead. When it turned gray before his death years later, I called it "Stalin hair" for the way it resembled the premier's. My father's eyebrows slanted toward the temples, giving him a perplexed look. After sailing the Great Lakes and the oceans, where, a wanderer, he'd visited Perth, Marseille, Mozambique and on postcards described the purple Arabian hills, how could he have ended up trapped sweeping floors in a flour mill, then coming home to a cold-water flat where a wife and two children waited? You know some have the potential to delight in the world, though not the opportunity. I saw little delight in Casimir Stasiak who, after he'd been home, lost his patience with my mother, brother Grzegorz, and me. Something was wrong when I saw Father that night in the snow, this tall, perplexed man with hollow cheeks and a mouth that turned down as though a grappling hook were pulling him back to where he'd once sunk.

A long time afterward I found out how ill he'd become. Roaming the phosphate docks of Casablanca or the native quarter of Old Medina where a million flies covered the meats of the vendors, he'd needed something more stimulating than the dance of Bou-Saâda to satisfy him. In Moroccan bazaars, scrawny fingers reached into his pockets. He was always a man of appetites. Was this how he got sick? With Bou-Saâda? Did *she* wonder whether certain kisses and touches were a sin? How often did Father return to her in the heat of the quarter? Dreaming of home as he lay beside her, perhaps he offered this dancer a Chesterfield. Besides a few of his postcards, I have some matches. On one box is an Arabic word, then a tiger silhouetted against a white moon. The stems of the matches are wax. I judge there to be thirty purple matches in the box our syphilitic father brought home. When I strike them in 1994, no flame.

He never told us about his infirmity. I heard from Mother. When he returned from the Arabian Sea, he informed her he wanted neither the arsenic-bismuth treatment nor fever therapy because in the age of disease a new treatment had been found.

What did I know except Mother never smiled? She couldn't escape the flat above the Coast-to-Coast store. Scandal started when wives left husbands. No gossips ever talked about Father, who was a hard worker during the time of disease and a member of St. Adalbert's Holy Name Society. Had Mother left with my brother and me, the gossipers surely would have said she'd had no cause to leave. So she endured Father to keep the talk from starting, to keep the nuns from whispering.

On the first page of a composition book from the maritime base at Fort Trumbull, New London, Connecticut, Casimir Stasiak had written, "Steps for Prevention of Venereal Disease." He should have followed them, but when theory became practice, my father, the sailor, the second assistant engineer, failed the course.

Now a thought that I, Franciszka (Stasiak) Thomasen, must always clarify to myself. Though a drunk, I am still not so callous as to attempt an analogy between my isolation and those who were quarantined during the war as "carriers of germs and epidemics." Only a fool would make a comparison between my sickness in a building where an old man yelled "Contagion!"—or between my father's sickness—and what happened on Polish soil. Still I must put down this family history, I must commit it. I'm a historian with three university degrees. Who better to tell about a sick man? I trust myself. I will make an effort starting with a kind of postcard of the past. Here is the awful, faded truth on the postcard: my immigrant ancestors' hatred and distrust survived the Atlantic crossing in the 1890s, then survived again when my father sailed back and forth from Baltimore to Fedallah or from New York to Casablanca during the war years. An ugly picture: Distrust. Hatred. We lived in a Polish neighborhood. It was 1945.

One of my aunts, she was a white-haired lady whose lap I'd sit on; one of my aunts would sing the "landlord song" I liked, then repeat stories over and over. There was one story about an incident on a bridge. She would say, "A wood bridge carry streetcar over river on Fourth Street. I'm on bridge once"—she'd say 'breedge'—"when Jew loose control of his wagon and horse. Somethink frighten horse. It jump up, get caught in railing, pull everythink over side. Jew, everythink."

Did he survive? I never knew. If he were an Archambeau, DeBruyne, or Gotelaere, would she say, "I was on bridge once when *Belgian* loose control of wagon"? Would she identify him the way she did the man with his wagon? Maybe they still talk like this in our neighborhood. Is it why the sick man hollers *"zarażenie"* in my ear today? Now I'm old with recollections. I didn't understand the ending to Auntie's story then. A Jew lost control of his wagon and that was it, the end of it? What kind of tale was that? Some of my family said other things. *I stumble about. I've spilled my drink. I cite a line from history: "According to the most careful estimates, about 3,350,000 Polish citizens of Jewish descent were slaughtered by the Nazis in Poland."*

Now Father was back, his friends home, war over (six million Jews killed in Poland and elsewhere), my brother, mother and grandmother waiting, his daughter found to be living in a pesthouse, and a job opened at the gas plant in Superior, Wisconsin. *Please help me someone. I'm drunk. I'm dying. I'll drink all night.*

3.

A month has passed since I've thought about it, tried to collect my thoughts. I've been in treatment. It goes day to day. Poor Hubert, my good husband, drove seventy miles to Shreveport to see me when he could. He grows exhausted caring for me, though. A dear husband, he teaches my college classes. My thinking's not straight. I have a disease. Poor Franciszka Stasiak in her dreams . . .

Has it been a month without reflection? For a historian, where I live is a good place. I drink on Bayou Amulet, think about history. In this way, I break the treatment they prescribe for me in Shreveport at the hospital: the abstinence from history, the abstinence from the bottle. Doctors tell me, "Don't think about your history all the time!" So I intoxicate myself with the past, fall down with it, find myself passed out with it on the back stoop of the sad house on the bayou.

With everyone returned by 1946, jobs needed filling. One opened at the Water and Light Company. Father felt qualified to be the "driver of a drip truck," which was the job title or description. When he applied, he took me, his poor, scarlet daughter, with him on the bus to the Water and Light Company.

"What does the job call for?" he'd asked the secretary.

"In a truck you go to natural gas mains, put a hose on them, then drip out water that's come in from condensation or in through porous pipes. We've not hired yet, Mr. . . . Mr. Stapik. You can fill out an application and call again," the lady'd said and gone back to her work.

"Thank you," he'd said in Polish. The secretary was probably Swedish. Here was my father now in somewhat reduced circumstances *bowing* to her. Bowing! I remember it. Was it a result of an illness? Did he think he was aristocratic? One of the *szlachta*, the nobility?

He'd go uptown every week to see whether he had the job. Never a sign of Casablanca or of Old Medina from him except he might lose his balance. When we returned to the flat, he'd ask whether Water and Light called Mrs. Callaway upstairs, who, since we had no phone, would relay the message to us.

As he sat alone in the kitchen searching the newspaper for other opportunities, he cleared his throat, smoothed his hair, I recall now, fearing him still. I didn't know whether there was "neurologic involvement." There wasn't in my case, I didn't think, but who knew for sure? My little brother would squirm away from me.

"Have you seen a doctor?" Mother would ask Casimir. She assumed I wasn't listening to them in the kitchen, that I was a child playing.

Folding his paper, he'd slap it on the table.

"Don't talk about doctors. Nothing's wrong here," he'd say.

Thinking he was straightening the tablecloth, he'd only leave it bunched at an angle. A portion of the table lay uncovered. When he called her "a spreader of idle tales," saying he was as healthy as the rest of us, she'd straighten the tablecloth, leave him mindlessly tapping the newspaper.

All that month no call came to Mrs. Callaway's flat with good news for Casimir Stasiak. No doubt there were many coincidences related to my father's not getting the Water and Light job. What if their newest employee, whose name we eventually learned was a Mr. Liebmann, had returned from the army a month later or had delayed his job application a day or two? Father may have had the job he wanted by then. But instead a coincidence occurred. Liebmann, Liebmann. A name entered our lives.

Like Liebmann's applying when he did, here is another coincidence I can't seem to forget—how in 1942 in a room off of an alcove in a dusty bazaar, a young Arab woman, Bou-Saâda, waited on an ottoman for Father with his purple matches, while in a room in the northeast section of Warsaw in 1944 another girl, maybe named Lottie or Clara, waited in terror for her German escorts, while here in America in 1946 in a room in an isolation hospital Franciszka Stasiak was beseeching St. Theresa to protect her. The pestilence was great all over. There was this triangle of children—one in a hospital here, one in an old quarter of Casablanca, one in a ghetto of Warsaw. If the last one survived, she was lucky. That *I* did was a coincidence, but what happened in the life of the daughter of a diminished man was that some of his infection spread. How did it happen that I should be infected, though not by the physical, venereal part of Casimir's life?

In those times of sickness and pain, an ad for the Water and Light Company read:

POWER FOR PROGRESS

A $52,000,000 expansion program since 1945 shows our faith in this great region of shipping, diversified industry, and recreation. It shows our confidence in the future . . . Providing POWER FOR PROGRESS.

Behind it was a drawing of hydroelectric generators and power lines. Everything was Progress . . . Liebmann . . . Progress. Dream shattered,

Casimir Stasiak ended up at the Fredericka Flour Mill where he swept grain dust from the packing floor. "It's like in the Old Country," Father told people in the Warsaw and Parrot taverns. He had the worst luck, was being kept down when he certainly *wanted* to join the march for progress. Now there was the name Liebmann, though.

With a nice drip truck, you bet Liebmann didn't have to walk. When Father drew the night shift was Liebmann out at 3 A.M. checking low-pressure gas mains? At daybreak, yellow with grain dust, Father would mutter *"Psia krew!* . . . Dog's blood!" as he stumbled home. I would go get him. Everywhere he turned, my father had lost out to progress—to Liebmann. Dogs nipped at his heels.

Maybe Liebmann had lived in town as long as we. Maybe like Father he, too, lost his patience, thought of the future, thought of the past, worried about bills as he sat in an undershirt at a kitchen table, argued with his wife, turned the calendar toward winter, laughed, played with his boy, took his family to movies when he had money. Wouldn't it be ironic to think we'd sat behind them at *Casablanca* with Humphrey Bogart or at *Morocco* with Charles Boyer? Now my father listened intently in the living room of the flat when our old aunt began her story of the rider on the bridge. "Tell it again, Auntie," he'd say, looking for other ancient reasons to dislike Liebmann. I've peeled away thinking about them.

4.

I am looking through a book, piecing thoughts together. In it, the writer is saying, "Poland is a country where, unfortunately—just as in America—one encounters a deep-rooted and evidently ineradicable anti-Semitism." Then he, Simon Wiesenthal, speaks of the "countless Poles who tried to help their Jewish compatriots" during the war. In fact, they saved his wife and him from death. Neither here nor in the Old Country should Poles be condemned. Many of our neighbors in

Superior would have fought for Liebmann. No one can say differently. If my father was hateful, such men live everywhere. With the neurological involvement he may have had, "infection of the brain leads to general paresis with psychoses and deterioration of the mental faculties." I could see the ranting worsen. He said Liebmann, no one and nothing but Liebmann, made him sick. Even in Casablanca, in Marseille . . . it was Liebmann who made him sick, he insisted.

I will call my thoughts now "Water and Light." In the back of Liebmann's truck (it is 1947) was a boilerlike tank where extracted water went. I'd see him working with his wrenches and his hammers around the neighborhood. Liebmann, a quick, lean Liebmann, was cooperative, energetic, efficient. Everything a company valued.

One day the nun led me to his truck. The sky looked bruised, it had turned so dark and hung so low over our rooftop. I'd been in church practicing crowning the Blessed Virgin, the Queen of the May, for Sunday's service, and there was a storm when I came out. Everyone ran. Sister Benitia called to Mr. Liebmann, "Can you take this little one a few blocks? You have your boy with you. Go on with Mr. Liebmann, Fronia," Sister said.

Mr. Liebmann pulled open the door. The cab smelled like the gas that utility companies warn you may escape from faulty stoves. The wind blew papers and dust about.

"Don't get yourself dirty in here. My boy's got piano lessons I've gotta take him to," he said.

Mr. Liebmann drew out a hankie, wiped the rain from his face. The boy Daniel sitting behind us was my age.

To this day I remember a wind tore pink and white blossoms from the trees so they looked like snowflakes building along the curb. I saw my father stumbling home, swinging his lunchbox at dogs and talking to himself. When he came in, I hardly recognized him—the red eyes, the vein in his neck nearly bursting.

Speaking softly, my mother said, "Casimir . . . if you throw down the lunchbox, you'll ruin the thermos."

"How'd you get home?" he asked me.

Flour flew up when he hit his fist on the table. "I walk home, see my daughter not notice me. She goes right by wit' her friends."

"Sister asked a man to drive me."

"She's a handmaiden to the Virgin today, Kazimierz," Mother was saying.

"Psia krew!"

I started to cry. If not for this history I'm recording, who'd remember my pesthouse? How easy to forget the Water and Light, too; these and other things—Auntie-storyteller's death, Mother's leaving Father when I was grown, my worsening infections in life—yes, my own, Franny Stasiak's. Here is my infection—thinking of the eighty-three thousand Polish Catholics murdered at Auschwitz. Why must we not care for the Catholics exterminated in those camps? Small numbers, eighty-three thousand, but should they be forgotten? *I am drunk, off course. Presidents, dignitaries . . . they will always say, "Six million Jews and 'others' were killed in the Nazi death camps in occupied Poland."* I've heard it often. There we are: "Others!" Always "Others." *I am off course. Steer me on course.* Who will bow to "others" if I don't? I bow to the humbler element, to the forgotten element! Is this an infection? *I'm drunk. Another college will let me go. There are no more. I've taught at every college—Central New Mexico, Missouri-Rolla, East Stroudsburg, Alverno.* Day in, day out, pestilence, pestilence. Most people up there in Superior, Wisconsin, aren't like me. Why is this an infection to remember Catholics killed at Auschwitz, Majdanek, and in the camps all over Poland?

Now in 1994 I pretend to be a child again. When I'd been a handmaiden and school was to close for summer, Mr. Liebmann—prized by the Water and Light Company—came by in his drip truck. I watched him until, finally, he said the strangest thing.

"You're Polish."

"Yes," I answered.

"Good," he said.

No one would compliment me on it again, I think. I'm sixty years old and surely would remember someone's compliment.

What did it mean that time? I wonder on a November midnight in 1994—no, 3 A.M. when I am so sick with this drunkenness I have. Fever and thirst. I remember them the way I do the picnic on the school grounds and Mr. Liebmann telling me it was good I was Polish. It's haunted me. I've studied numbers over the years and found that the Poles, Gypsies, intellectuals, the disabled, the homosexuals killed at Auschwitz and elsewhere are called "Others." Was Mr. Liebmann remembering them or remembering those heroes whom Wiesenthal wrote about, "the countless Poles who tried to help their Jewish compatriots" during the war? *O God, must I worry that we're called "Others"? Am I sick with resentment that I argue about the dead and defend Polish suffering and want it acknowledged? Eighty-three thousand Polish Catholics died at Auschwitz alone. I offer them my small bows.*

There was, in memory, this isolation hospital. Its chimney smoke rose above the neighborhood.

Innocently, a half-century ago, I told Mother at supper during the first snow after a hard, November rain, "Daniel Liebmann is quarantined."

Coming into the kitchen, Casimir Stasiak said, "How do you know this, Franny?"

"Sometimes he's in the truck with him when he comes by school, but not now anymore, so I asked Mr. Liebmann."

"You can't be reinfected," Mother said. "There's nothing left to peel away."

"She is reinfected. *I* can't breathe either. Don't say Liebmann. I get sick. You come here," my father was saying, yelling.

Mother grabbed him as he pulled on his work coat. He was syphilitic. He threatened her, swore at her. He went through the flat looking for my coat. Throwing clothes from closets, he told me that any disease around there came from me. He threatened to hit Mother if she didn't get away from us.

"I don't want to go," I'd said. (Sometimes I still say it. Then Hubert wakes me and quiets me.)

My father grabbed my collar. "You're reinfected so bad?" he asked in Polish.

From the landing upstairs, Mrs. Callaway watched as Father pulled me out the door, past Dunalski's, past the icehouse, past the railroad freight depot on Tenth Street. When he let go of my arm, he weaved on alone down the road, turning periodically to wave me on. Dogs chased after him.

An iron gate read ISOLATION HOSPITAL. Light snow covered the fields as it had when Father came home. High up in the brick and stone of the building stood a soot-blackened arch pigeons flew into. Far below, a glass panel, a religious painting, decorated the entryway, part of the sorrowful mysteries of a place where people were isolated. Christ was isolated.

Now a syphilitic cursed his isolation, cursed a Jew, then cursed Liebmann's son, who, waving innocently, pressed his face to a third-floor window the way I had once done.

Out of the neighborhood toward the isolation hospital the drip truck came.

"Liebmann!" Father called as he saw it. "You . . . your kid. We're tired of infection."

Surprised, Mr. Liebmann must have wondered who was this yelling at him?

"Don't, Father."

I saw a nurse in the upstairs window beside Daniel.

Picking up a brick that'd probably fallen from the walls and lain there in the mud for a year, Father tossed it at Mr. Liebmann. If I trust myself, if I value myself despite my weakness, I must believe that this brick smashed out the corner of the Lamb of God. Glass lay over the threshold of the hospital.

"Praised be Jesus Christ!" yelled Father. "Right now," he said, yanking me. "You spit there, Jewess. You spit on him for his truck." He slapped me. I wouldn't do it. My father—my dear, hated father—spit at Mr. Liebmann of the Water and Light, calling him words I'd never heard, resenting him for his drip truck.

For my history, I'd put it about November 13 that Mr. Liebmann picked up a piece of the broken glass, turned away, and walked inside. Why did Casimir the syphilitic think Liebmann couldn't enter a pesthouse? What was going to hurt him when sometimes fifteen thousand a day had come in boxcars to Auschwitz, fifteen thousand Jews?

Of the neighborhood where we lived, a person could say in a history like mine that in the fall of 1947 a man had been harassed. He'd shown Liebmann all right! my father told everyone. "Sure I had to put him in his place," he said, weaving on to the next tavern as smoke from rags and dressings wound from The Pesthouse chimneys.

By St. Francis's Day, that would be the third of December, Daniel Liebmann, who'd recovered, wrote me a note. He'd drawn a delicate sketch of the isolation hospital. From the school window, I watched for his father.

Winter came. An odd neighborhood, I could hear polkas playing when it was twelve below zero. Before the flat I lived in, snow swept down the street. The bay and the town froze. Everyone stayed inside, but I could hear the polkas drifting through the alleys.

My father reread newspapers he'd brought home from his journeys—the *Basrah* and *Iraq Times*, the *Lourenço Marques Guardian*, "Moçambique's Oldest Newspaper." He'd go on about the old days, dully though, as if stupefied by a midday sun on the Arabian Sea. "What's this?" Mother once asked about a photo of a Moroccan dancer.

I graduated from St. Adalbert's School. During the winter holiday of my second year at East High School when through the crisp air I could hear the loudspeaker at the skating rink playing "White Christmas" as I sat quietly in the kitchen dreaming of places I'd like to visit, Mother called from the bedroom, "Look, Franciszka, at The Pesthouse." The third floor where I'd peeled away was burning. The blazing hospital eclipsed the moon. Before I pulled down my shade on the sicknesses filling the burnt sky, I imagined the silhouette of the lives of people who could hate each other. I imagined the silhouette of Father spitting at Mr. Liebmann. The fire lit up East End, and the silhouettes went marching over it. I will write it down in my history that Mr. Liebmann had had the Lamb of God repaired.

Years later by accident I saw a human being's cremated remains. I'd gone to a crematorium with a friend when I taught at Grand Canyon College in Phoenix. Another friend was picking up an uncle who'd wished to be disposed of this way. How hot must have been the oven to reduce a human to ash, I thought. It was a pile of bone and ash a child could hold in his palms. How much hotter than the fire at The Pesthouse that'd gotten out of hand before I closed my shade. Though I'm old now, I see The Pesthouse burning.

Curiously, thinking of Phoenix in my sickness reminds me of a teaching job my husband and I held at a college in Pennsylvania. There I had a friend named Florence in the history department who invited me to lunches and parties. With my last name being Thomasen, she didn't know I was Polish. Hers was Florence Rubenfield. In the history office after lunch one day, six or seven of us were laughing and talking. How did the topic of ancestry come up? Everyone started saying what they were: Swedish, Norwegian . . . When my turn came, I threw up my arms. "I'm a noble Pole," I announced.

Florence stopped laughing. Her face turned ash gray. "Ask my relatives about noble Poles," she said coldly. This was my last lunch date with Florence Rubenfield.

So forty-eight years ago when I was young, a man immune to infection walked into a pesthouse to visit his son. Let me not make so much of it in my history of disease when I don't know how much I myself have contracted of the ancestral sickness. I do know that just as there were honorable Poles during the war, so, too, were there Jews like Liebmann after the war who were good to remember our suffering.

5.

I haven't thought as often of Mr. Liebmann and his son the past few nights. How do I tell myself to finish with them? The man who tormented himself over Mr. Liebmann has been dead twenty-seven years now, leaving me his purple matches. My mother, too, is gone; someone is saying a rosary for her. How do I finish telling myself about Liebmann, then retelling it all my life?

He will always be part of me. So will the Polish neighborhood I will drink out of my mind if I can. About myself I ask this: Had I loved the Jew who said "good" when I told him who I was? Yes, I did—for his kindness, for his patience, for his courage in walking away from Father. Though he is out of my thoughts for a month at a time, I never unchain myself from the man who worked for Water and Light. Maybe this, after all, is why I lose so many jobs, because I remember postcards of Mr. Liebmann and the Lamb of God, of Edda Wasko, and of Father before he sailed away. Mr. Liebmann was everything at the Water and Light, and he is the only one who saved me in those days.

"Poland and the Jews . . . tell us about them," my better students say. I have a hard time doing so, because I never understood hatred. I do understand the intricacies of hearts that don't belong, however. With these I'm quite intimate. I know that once when I was sober I heard people chanting in a park in Boston, "The People of Israel Live!"; that once I knew a Florence Rubenfield who'd lost people in the war and in the Nazi extermination camps; and that once I saw an oven in the desert and now myself have chosen that means of disposal. Hubert, my husband, will arrange it when my time comes. Then will be returned to ash a heart that didn't belong.

I would go by The Pesthouse now in winter if I were there in Superior. I'd clear away the snow. Walk the foundation. Nothing has been built on the spot, I know. I wish tonight I could go to the place to discover for my history what I still can of the intricacies of certain hearts' workings. I wish someone could write to me to inform me whether in spring the creeks and ravines will still run muddy up there in Superior, Wisconsin, or write to inform me that no flowers or shrubs grow on The Pesthouse grounds.

For me (alone in Louisiana with my sickness tonight), I try to remember Polish, but the only Polish words I remember anymore— words for "pesthole," for "pestiferous"—bring with them memories of my father in the native quarter of Old Medina or on the phosphate docks of Casablanca.

Dry Spell

1.

THE FIRST DRY HOURS

The long drive to the last Catholic church in Superior has been hard for Mrs. Koudelka. Now she leaves the car at home and walks to my neighbor Jacek "Jack" Zukowski's house. Once a deacon (and the closest thing to a priest in these parts), he specializes in spiritual healing and reconciliation. I've heard him telling sinners, "Confess to one another, and pray for one another, so that you may be healed. If you sin, then pull the confessional curtain back. Come in and confess."

"Thank you," old women say in Polish when Jacek absolves them. Passing my place pure of heart, they raise their hands in prayer. Teenage girls and county road workers come up the road to forgiveness, too. With the churches closed, where else to get penance and absolution?

Out on County W, Jacek has a sign:

CONFESSIONS HEARD THURSDAYS, MAY TO SEPTEMBER

4:30 TO 7 P.M.

Nowadays you can buy cut-rate pews, half-price baptismal fonts, discount vestments, organs, and altar cloths. Even confessionals are easy to come by. For sitting in his own private confessional with a beer in hand, Jacek earns thirty to forty dollars a month whispering to people, "Go and sin no more," then reminding them to visit the "Grove of Saints" on their way out and to please leave an additional offering in the alms box.

When the water-well trouble starts, however, Jacek Zukowski has to close down confessions.

He calls me as I'm telling Tami, my wife, how I was recommended for the Medal of Honor, but didn't get it because the Joint Chiefs of Staff screwed up the paperwork. I was a Vietnam fighter pilot, a POW.

"I've never seen wounds on you, Simmy," she says.

"Let's not talk about wounds now," I tell her. "I've got wounds."

Checking my faucets, flushing my toilet, I call Jacek back to tell him I'll be right over to see about the well we share.

Because it's boggy in the woods, I walk the road to Wonderland, which is what I call Jacek's because of the interesting things he has in his yard. The lane off "W" into his place winds through aspen and poplar. Eight plaster statues of St. Margaret, St. Rose of Lima, St. Ann de Beaupré, St. Joseph, St. Patrick, St. Stanislaus, the Sacred Heart, and St. Bernadette, who saw Our Lady of Lourdes, stand on pine stumps in there. They are life-sized. He bought them at church going-out-of-business sales. Once past the saints, the lane turns a little toward the confessional, which is made of polished brown wood with a crucifix rising over the center part, before straightening out and stopping beside the barn, where hang the fourteen Stations of the Cross.

"How do?" he says, getting up from genuflecting at the second station: JESUS BEARS HIS CROSS.

"Workday. I can't stay. Where's the trouble, Jacek?" I ask him.

"I think it's a break in our water line, Simmy," Jacek mutters. He figures the pipe curves between the house and the barn, then to the well where, if the pump keeps running, the motor will burn up. Jacek will be without holy water if it does, and we will be without the regular water that runs a tenth-mile from his well pump to our faucets, which is also how far I come for spiritual redemption. As Jacek and I look for wet ground, two dogs trot up. "Hey," I say as they peer around the side of the barn.

Jacek calls friendly-like to them, "What you boyce doing here? What you do here?"

"They want confession," I say. "Sinners. Sinning dogs."

Maybe my uniform scares them off, the Midwest Security shoulder patch and badge, the big chest of the little five-foot-zero Simmy. Maybe my neighbor's accent or his brown workboots, khaki workpants, and canvas jacket scare them, or Jacek's size scares them. He's big, heavyset, fat in the stomach, though his belly isn't as bad as many you see around here. He's wound a key chain around his pants button, then down through the eyelet of his pants zipper to keep it pulled up, but it doesn't work. The zipper hangs halfway open.

Before he telephoned me with his water-line business, I was having breakfast in bed, telling Tami about the Medal of Honor and reading to her how Wisconsin residents are the fattest in the country. The paper says it's because of two things: the "genetic disposition" of people from north and east Europe like Jacek Zukowski plus the bitter winters that keep a person indoors. Jacek isn't too fat except in the belly. His wrinkled face, where lines sweep beside his eyes and mouth, makes it look like he wears a mask.

"Is this water here, Simmy?" asks Jacek.

When I signal no, he says, *"Psia krew,"* spitting at the clay.

"How do you pronounce it in Polish, 'shaw kref'?"

Before he answers, he enters the confessional and pulls the curtain behind him. When he kneels I see his boots and pants legs. "Lord forgive me for cursing," he says. A minute later, out comes Jacek mumbling penance, blessing himself. He's forgiven his own sin, forgiven himself for saying *"psia krew."*

"What's so bad about what you said?"

"It's bad," he says. "When I was a young Jacek and asked what it meant, the relatives said, 'Don't you say those curse words in a-house, you.' Now that I'm an old man, I know what they mean."

"You aren't even sixty-five. You're Polish. You're strong."

"'Dog' is *psia*," Jacek says, pulling at the key chain. "*Krew* is 'blood.' The words don't mean exactly that though. It's not 'dog's blood,' but 'God's Blood.' It got changed around to mean that during some century in the past. It's a curse that once meant 'dog's blood.'"

Despite the cursing, he's doing pretty good with fifteen autos, seven or eight rusting refrigerators, a broken Maytag wringer-washer, an old wooden motorboat resting on sawhorses in the yard, big hole punched in the side. A pile of bricks rises beside the barn. He has sinners marching in, Little Simmy next door, a pile of weathered boards— enough to build a shed—lying beneath a canvas tarp. He collects it all. Hanging inside the barn is a picture of two fat workmen sitting on the grass with a naked lady. It's by this foreign artist Jerzy Duda-Gracz. A lot of junk collectors live in Douglas County, Wisconsin, though none hears confessions or collects great art.

When he spits again, the spit lands on wet soil. "It must be the break over here," he says. He aims a shovel at the outer edge of the small, damp circle in the clay.

"*This* what you mean by *psia krew?*" I ask.

"It's martyred, mysterious bleeding. Shut the pump off. I'll go in, call someone to look at the well," he says.

I watch the arrow on the pressure gauge fall to 40, 30, 20 when I shut off the pump. This is mine and Tami's falling pressure.

2.

WELL AGREEMENT

When Jacek comes out of the house after making the phone call, he's carrying a bag of crushed beer cans he's found in the ditch along the

Military Road and will bring to Zimko Recycling in town. The car will be loaded with cans when he leaves, and after a few hours he'll return drunk. "I sell nine bags, get forty bucks," Jacek will tell us, complaining about the recycling man. "'Why you goddamn Zimko!' I felt like saying to him, 'I can get twice as much for these cans someplace else.'"

Being a collector he's soon back along the roadside looking for beer cans or driving the county, collecting. By nightfall he'll have maybe another broken refrigerator, another bag of cans, a toilet or toilet tank, a trailer with a broken hitch and bald tires, a bathtub, a sign that reads "Prime Steer Steakhouse" or "East End Cafe," even one day the tall wooden confessional with the torn curtains on it where he sits sliding the screens back and forth and where he once heard me say, "I ain't been intimate in twelve years."

"Whoa, Simmy. How can she go without? Not for 144 months! You sure?"

"We never talk about it. Guess we don't think about it much till someone cracks a joke on TV about married couples and how many times a week they never do it. Then we laugh and get uncomfortable as we recall the twelve dry years we never made love."

That time Jacek was already giving me penance to calm me down, but my soul got out of control and, revved up, I kept confessing. "I'm 'Big Simmy, Security Man.' But at home I have no interest in venery."

"That's deer meat," Jacek said.

"No, venery's sexual desire. College taught me that," I told him. I smelled his beer breath through the confessional screen. "It hurts that I've never laid-hand on her in love but only right after we were married. Don't ever tell no one when you're out collecting. If they heard about the absence of venery, they'd laugh. I'm a security man with badge, walkie-talkie, and nightstick. I don't like laughing. Reputation's important in this business," I said to him.

* * *

As I leave down the lane now, up pulls the truck. The driver's been looking at fire numbers on the Military Road. "FJORD WELL DRILLING   Steve T. Bienek   WATER IS OUR BUSINESS," the side of the cab reads.

"This the well trouble with a broken line?"

"Over here's Jacek," I tell him and keep going toward home and toward work on the docks. The two sinning dogs, having important plans, watch me out of the side of their eyes.

At home Tami in a negligee slides between me and the bedroom door as I check my look in the mirror hanging from it. Simmy sees his high forehead, his deep-set eyes, his pug nose, firm chin . . . Simmy sees his large head and neck, broad shoulders that represent the authority that is "Security Simmy," former POW and screwed-up Medal of Honor winner.

"Here," Tami says. She's naked now. The mirrored door hits my arm as she walks out of the bedroom. "Give us a kiss." She bends down to a twelve-year failure. I'm shorter than her.

"No kiss. Pressure's falling. No kissing or touching me."

"Why?"

"Broken water pipe, I think. If you need Jacek to turn on the pump, call him when the water-well guy leaves. He'll have to keep the pump off most of the time until the break gets fixed or water will keep running out. No kissing or touching."

Grabbing my keys, I slide the screen door shut. From over at Jacek's I hear talking. We'll be waterless, but at least the break is on his property. The Well Agreement we made when we moved in (so we wouldn't have to drill a well and Jacek wouldn't have to pay if his went bad) read, "Jacek Zukowski hereby assigns and conveys to Arnold Simpson, his heirs, successors and assigns, an undivided one-half (½) interest in and to the above mentioned well, casing, pump, motor, and related equipment, and the right to take water from the well for his own domestic purposes. The parties will share the well, together with all expenses, equally." I can't see this means paying for repairs on something next to *his* house, though.

When I ride past, Bienek the well man is gesturing, shovel in hand. There are the brick piles, the moat of old cars, the castle wall of refrigerators and washers, Prince Bienek and the khaki-clad King Jacek in the yard staring at clay, knowing something has given way, the waterless mansion behind—a haunted, spiritual palace. I drive by again, see Bienek following Jacek Zukowski to confession.

3.

THE FOURTH DRY HOUR

In town the lake wind blows dirt and dust. It was a boomtown once. Iron ore got shipped out of here, wheat, timber. A railroad and shipping center, it's what they call "the western terminus of the Great Lakes." Along Tower Avenue, newspapers, dead leaves, and cigarette butts tumble toward Oakes and Banks Avenues. Beer cans roll toward the 21st Street tracks. Everyone living in the dirt and wind here is left over or hung over—from a business that failed, from a marriage that failed, from a church that closed, from a drinking bout, from general unhappiness. A sign put up for tourists reads: "In 1953, 32.3 million tons of iron ore were shipped from our docks." That was forty-four years back. Not much goes out now in 1997.

On the sides of buildings are faded signs for the Finnish paper *Työmies Eteenpäin*, for Polish butchers, fish-packing warehouses, railroad and tourist hotels, old, failed establishments still advertising on vacant buildings. Around the mills and docks, dust-monitoring stations, gray and fenced-in, stand alone in the middle of empty fields where nothing interferes with readings of what our air holds. On metal legs four feet high, the instruments measure lime, ore, coal dust. Everything's dirty in a town that's permanently out of order. Now a dust monitor stands on the lot where Jacek's Polish church once stood. His Polish Club is closing.

Tami calls me. "Jacek told me the well man's phoning all over. He can't get a backhoe driver for a few days yet."

"I'll bring drinking water out home when I come. I gotta go."

A half-hour from the desert of my marriage, I work Harvest States Grain Elevator, watching for trespassers, listening for high school kids shooting rats with .22s. All shift I drive around or walk below grain silos. On the other side of the silos, beyond four sets of railroad tracks that run the length of the dock, twelve more connected silos stand. This is the security business.

I check the rail yard. A locomotive idles, no one in it. A half-block north, a bridge carries traffic to Duluth. Sometimes pigeons squawk and flap about. Sometimes water drips on me. At the base of the silos, bollard posts line the half-mile pier. From the edge of the sky to the bottom of the slip atop which lakers and ocean boats ride—how far, Simmy? How far would it be from here to there, from sky to harbor bottom— as deep as if you fell into the truth and finally knew about yourself that you weren't in war and that you don't like touching and kissing?

I need a depth gauge. In clay country, wells are three hundred feet deep. Water drips on me. This endless driving and walking about. Forty-five minutes per round, then start in again. On the forty-sixth minute, I, Arnold "Simmy" Simpson, five-foot-zero-inches tall, thirty-eight years old and of sound mind, stop in at the yard office for a drink of water from the cooler.

"How's the nuts today?" I ask the grain trimmers on break. Wheat husks hanging from his eyelids, Clarence Fiandt grabs a bag of peanuts from the vending machine.

"Salty. How's urine?" he says.

"Salty."

We go through the same routine every day. I want to smile at the joke. *Little Simmy wants to laugh.* But thinking life is a dead end, I grow quiet. Half a shift left before I go back fourteen miles to a broken water pipe. I feel like four-foot-nine.

"Gotta call in," I tell him.

"*Hasta la* bye-bye," Clarence says. "So long, Shorty."

"Come back when you can't stay, Half-Pint," Ray Eliason says.

"I won't," I tell them. "I'm in dry dock, roaming the desert."

Shoulders back, I swagger before the window of the Midwest Security van. "Simmy" Simpson. Unloved, dry-balled Simmy the BS-er, five-foot-two or shorter. "Watch out for Simmy," I say, combing my hair, checking my zipper like Jacek Zukowski does.

I drive a road between silos. I sit on a booster pillow. I lean forward, raising up off the pillow when I spot someone, a drunk woman stumbling. One part of her tan raincoat hangs from her shoulder.

"Frien's lef me," she says when I roll down the window. "Can I catch a ride? They're at the Anchor Bar."

"What you doing? It's private property. I've talked to all you girls about it before."

"Italian boat's come in. Captain had a party," she says. "We've been drinking with the captain of the *La Boheme*. I'll pay. Can you ride me to the Anchor?"

She hands me a box.

"What's in it?"

"Soap."

"Laundry soap?" I say. "Lookit the writing. It's probably Italian."

"Captain give me one. All I have to pay with. No, this too," she says, handing me a hundred rubles she must've gotten on a Russian boat.

"Get in. Don't get sick in here."

"What you doing riding around? Yer like a shrimp." She can hardly talk. A string of hair falls across her nose. "M'name's Jill."

"I'm the head of a government office," I tell her. "Special work."

When I glance over, her head slumps sideways to the window. I go on talking, telling her I was with the Wisconsin State Patrol, the Immigration and Naturalization Service, now with a special government office. I tell her I have a black belt in karate, a Medal of Honor. She sleeps. She don't care about it. Maybe she needs confession.

Pretending to open her window to give her some air, I touch her. She raises her arm to stop me but, drunk, lets it fall. I touch the front of her blouse again, trace the edge of bra beneath, feel myself get bigger on the booster pillow. I raise up to look. I think of the picture in Jacek's barn of the naked woman in this string bikini-thong contraption having a picnic lunch with the two fat workmen. In the shadow of a silo, I touch her again. I touch her face. My elbow hits the horn. The noise echoes off silos. "My name's Lulu," she says and stirs. "My name's not Jill."

"Did I tell you I have a black belt in karate and was a weight lifter in the 1992 Tucson Olympics? No, the San Mateo Olympics."

"There wasn't any. Who are you? What you doin' here?" she asks, looking around like she can't remember getting in. "I musta fell asleep. What's your real name? Yer just a cocktail shrimp."

"Bienek," I tell her when I drop her off at the Anchor.

4.

SACRAMENT OF PENANCE

We go four days using water from plastic jugs to wash and shave with, four days pissing out beer under the cold May stars with the wood frogs and peepers coming to life, four days with Tami telephoning Jacek, asking, "Can you run the pump a few minutes so my husband can clean up?" The neighbor's saints guard us all.

"Bienek can't get a backhoe driver. All heavy equipment in the world is busy," Jacek says over the phone. "Let's keep the pump off a little more or water seeps up from the break."

We can see him through the brush, a lonely man moving junk around in his blue jacket and khaki clothes.

When I visit, he's sitting inside the confessional. "Save the can for me?" he says. He hands me a beer. "Anything to confess for two dollars?"

I forget the woman on the docks. All I did was touch her.

"No, I been good. What do you suppose about the well, Jacek?"

"Guy's afraid of water . . . gets hydrophobic when he's in a hole watching water run out of broken pipe. I tole him it's a mortal sin for a well man to be hydrophobic."

"No BS?"

"I wouldn't BS you, you're my favorite turd," he says, then shrugs. "Oops." He kneels in confession, comes out forgiven, smiling. "I'd like some of his plumbing stuff," he says. "I'd run water to the confessional."

"Be sure to use copper pipe if you do. Don't use lead, Jacek. You'll have lead in your holy water."

"Won't matter. You only use it to bless yourself. By the way, I said 'psia krew' again."

"Why this time?"

"Don't know. Just for everything. I'll be buried rotten under this stuff, but anything goes haywire, I got the parts for it at least. I got the saints at different places. I bought the confessional when they tore down St. Clem's. I paid a month's worth of aluminum for it. It's a loss of faith in the world. Churches all gone everywhere. Nobody has faith, Simmy. As a kid I went to confession all-a time. There's nothing for me to confess now if you don't believe in anything. Even in Poland, a Roman Catholic country, people are losing the faith."

"There's a dust monitor station at your old church, Jacek. I have fears, too. Afraid of I'll be small and little all my life and have to make up for it by BS-ing and stretching the truth to make myself big. Look at me. I'm four-foot-two."

"God's Blood is shed for us every day, Sim. It's no mystery. The Blood of Christ drips due to sorrow in the world. Man's wrongdoing causes it. Lookit how the pipe has broken and the well man ain't come. Lookit Zimko gone haywire with low aluminum prices. Lookit the rain going to start, the wild dogs. Lookit the ten Catholic churches closing in Superior. These are maybe little things amounting to a drop of blood, but they add up over centuries into 'God's Blood.' When people hang on to stuff like I got, they're hoping for self-preservation. If you're self-sufficient you save up things. When the time comes, you yourself fix what's gone wrong with yourself. I'm a survivalist. A soul survivalist."

"I can't fix what's gone wrong with me, and you can't fix our water line, Jacek."

"It'd kill me at my age to dig in clay, Simmy. Anyway, I have what I need to fix *my* problems." He raps on the confessional's wooden wall. "Kneel down. I'll hear your confession free."

"Jacek," I say as he pulls back the screen, "this is hard to tell you. I've never said it to anyone. I don't love my wife."

"Don't get to the sin right off. Say 'Bless me, Jacek.' Now tell how long since your last confession."

My soul is jumping with the thrill of confession and repentance, the thought of being reconciled to God through Jacek.

"Hold it. When you get to the sin, don't use words like 'several times' or 'quite often.' Count them exactly. This is the Blood of a-Christ we're dealing with."

"*Psia krew,*" I say. "If I wasn't so short, I'd feel better about things. You know my real height? Three-foot-one. No, three-foot-zero."

I sip a beer. He returns my whispers. "Have you taken pleasure in impurity? Is that it? Willful impurity?"

"Yes."

"Where, please?"

"In the truck, the van, I mean, where kissing and touching's allowed."

"Who was it, please?"

"A woman come down to the docks to make money. I've seen two carloads pull up to the boats at a time. They go aboard, have parties, make moola. This one was walking back to North Third Street. She said the captain couldn't steer his ship. She wanted love and was willing to pay and even give up her Fond-du-Luth Casino jacket. She said it was pretty big on Little Simmy. Simmy ain't so little. Simmy's pretty big, Jacek. She gave me her bingo winnings. Fifty dollars."

"Whoa, geezus, that's a lot of aluminum. I don't know about all this, Simmy," Jacek says.

"Can't afford not to get paid for it. Made two thousand dollars last year. I didn't declare it on my taxes, so don't say anything. What would I file it under, Love Income? Women down there call me 'Big Simmy–Security Man.' With Tami, though, I don't go anywhere near her. A twelve-year failure, that's me. Jacek, can you give me credit in confession for venery I don't use at home so I can store it up for future use on the docks?"

"I don't see how," he says, then blesses and gives me penance. "Go and sin no more," he tells me.

5.

DETERGENT

When on the fifth dry day (in the twelfth year without venery), Mr. Bienek still doesn't come, Tami wakes me from the well of sleep. I worked the midnight shift.

"There's no water *yet*. Feels like years," she says.

"Why'd you say that? I work hard. I'm tired. It must be my blood pressure medicine I take that I can't provide for your needs. Did you know I was a doctor once?"

When I see her, I think how I shouldn't have confessed what I confessed to Jacek: the secret. I wonder whether a person can take *back* confession. "Can you wash my clothes?"

"Without water?" she asks. "Where'd this detergent come from?"

"I don't know. Did I tell you the well man's hydrophobic?"

"I want water," she says.

"Is Jacek outside?"

"He's moving stuff. Simmy, please go catch him."

On the road I see the dogs. A new, light-colored one trots in front. "Where've you been? I don't recognize you from around here. You visiting Wonderland?" I ask.

When he gets closer, I see a scarlet chin, red nose: God's Blood. He and the other two dogs veer away from me into the woods, maybe embarrassed at being spotted going wild. But only one of the three dogs has blood.

"When do we get water?" I ask Jacek from up the lane near the Grove of Saints. I thrust out my chest. After years of bragging, I am just a chest talking, no head, no mouth, no chin.

"We can't have water."

"Why? I gotta get my clothes washed from the 'Big Simmy' business I did in them the other night. I want to take back what I said in confession. I'll give you two dollars to let me take it back."

"No, you can't take back something like sin. Watch for the dogs. They're back in there," he says, pointing to a path through the deep brush.

"They're hounding me," I say.

"All right, then I'll take back your sins, but the new rite costs six dollars."

Kneeling, whispering, I say to the confessional screen, "Bless me, Jacek. We have venery all the time at our trailer."

"How often?"

"At least twelve times per week."

"Every mont'?"

"Yup. Twelve times per week except on December 20 or 21. That's an extra three times because of all the darkness." I feel the man-sized chest expand and press against the confessional. Expanded, it grows hard for me to breathe. The Simmy-Chest blows up, puffs up, and Jacek must pull me by the collar to get my chest out of confession.

"Am I absolved? Are my sins taken back?"

"Not yet. You haven't gotten penance."

"Where you pulling me? You know I'm not a little Simmy. I'm no one-foot-nine or nothing. Heck, I wouldn't even need that booster pillow at work. Here, in my wallet . . . Russian money to pay you with. Heck, you bet. It's the regular income of a satisfied man."

"Fix your zipper. Come on. Your chest is so big and puffed out with pride that it's going to take a lot of instruction to get 'er back to a reasonable size. Grab your booster pillow at home if you need it."

"Where we goin'?"

"In here," he says, pointing beyond the path through the thick brush to a grove of birches.

"You been here, Jacek? I've never seen you come from in here."

"It's a sanctuary. Some sin requires special penance. I think you just might be having too much venery with your wife. That can be sinful, too."

Brushing aside aspen saplings and alder, he tells me it gets swampy underfoot. "Watch it," he says. "T'row back the shoulders. Arch the back. In t'rough here, push out your chest."

"I am. It's adding inches to me. I've got a lot of authority. I'm no lonely, BS-ing Simmy walking here."

"What?"

"I say I was a POW fighter pilot in the war."

"A *what?*"

"A gigolo that makes money at love on the grain docks."

"Say again?"

"I was a doctor once, Jacek. Did I tell you I performed open heart surgery?"

"Simmy, you aren't even self-sufficient of the spirit, which is the first step to happiness. Lookit me, your Jacek. I confess, I absolve, I

anoint myself with Last Rites when I'm not feeling good and am afraid
of dying young. With so many churches going under, soon there won't
be priests or religious left anywhere. You have to do for yourself nowadays," he says. "And you're not doing for yourself."

Bending, he uses both arms to push the brush back. We're deeper
than I want to go. There could be quicksand, snipers, VC.

"Geezus! Whoa," I say, like Jacek does, when I see why he's brought
me. These eight I've never seen before are life-sized plaster statues, too.
Shy, pious, they stare out at me from the tamaracks like the ones in the
lane do. They're all from closed churches.

"Whoa yourself. Make a sign of the cross," Jacek says.

I do. "In the name of the Father . . ."

"Including the statues in the lane, this makes sixteen I own. Here's
St. Hedwig. I got her in Stevens Point," he says. "Here's St. Theresa of
the Child Jesus from a Minneapolis church. Here's your St. Nympha,
your Maria Goretti, many of them virginal ones noted for the absence
of venery. They got some miles on 'em. I've hauled them in my backseat from as far as Davenport, where everything's closed down tight. No
Catholic churches left."

"So *this* is finally *psia krew?*"

"Not *psia krew* yet, Sim. Here, come on in behind the tamaracks a
little more."

"Ho-lee!" I say.

"You bet holy," says Jacek.

Afraid to look, I feel sick when I do. The dark, brown, dead eyes
stare up sadly. The deer's carcass has been gnawed. The one dog, the tan
one, is at the chest now. The two black dogs are full of blood.

"Things seem more direct with these boyce. The boyce run down
weak deer, kill them, feed right on the blood with the crows and other
eaters. Humans create sin but don't taste God's Blood. When the wild
boyce eat right in front of us what they found, they are a lesson to us
about His Body. Boyce eat the deer's body. But the statues? No, they're
pure and holy representations, and nobody touches them."

"*Psia krew!* God's Blood!"

"You bet. The eating and tasting is a symbol of the pouring out of Christ's life. It's all got to do with self-sufficient. You're not self-sufficient, Simmy-lad. Me, for instance. I'll wait around, say a novena. Maybe later today I'll call again in here. I'll get what's left of everything. Some of that meat's probably good. Later on, I'll confess to myself for anything I might-a done, then absolve or anoint myself. Why not? No churches to go to."

"No BS?"

"No BS. With these dogs hounding us, it's important to maintain a state of grace. It's important for you, too, in the dry spell you're in. Nobody believes in anything anymore."

"Jesus, Jee-zus, Jacek! It makes me sick that I'm a dry-balled, sinful liar."

"Sick's what sin makes you. God's Blood don't drip, it flows for us, bursts. God bursts."

"Simmy? Simmy?" I hear my wife—the wife I've denied for twelve dry years—calling from over in the lane. "Tell Jacek to turn on the water so we can wash your work clothes. Ask him when the well man's coming with a backhoe driver."

"This makes me so sick, Jacek," I tell him. "A dead deer. The dogs eating."

"The boyce like the taste. It's a holy place we're in. We're survivalists. I better remember a piece of that for my supper, too. Maybe I'll go have a picnic. Hey, don't sin, but if you do, Simmy, I'll confess you. I'm glad you believe. I'm glad you're surviving a modern world of fear so well."

"Jesus," I say back. "That I ain't touched her must be one of the 'sorrowful mysteries' of the blood."

"Well, if it is, then bring her over here for a picnic of repentance and forgiveness at Jacek's. There's always plenty to go around. When we're done we can see about that hydrophobic well man."

"Jesus . . . *Jesus!*" I say and stumble out through the brush tunnel and down the sacred lane of traveling saints from all over the Midwest. The bloody dog runs beside me. I am dry-balled, and I hear her at our place calling, "Ask Jacek when the well man's coming. Tell Jacek we need water to wash your stinking clothes."

"I will, I will," I yell back to her. "Oh, God," I say to the bloody dog that nips at my cuffs and leaves the Blood of Christ on them.

The Absolution of Hedda Borski

I have prepared the bread and cotton when the priest arrives a little after eight. He's said Mass at St. Adalbert's and come over. We have coffee.

"Your house looks very nice," he says. "Do you live downstairs? Where's your sister?"

"In her bedroom." I can hear her up there shuffling things on the nightstand. "She takes medicine for an enlarged heart," I tell him. "She hasn't been downstairs in ten years."

"My heart can't take it," she says when we're halfway up the stairs to see her. "Tell him that, too, Julia! I hear you coming."

I carry up the table with the candlesticks, bread, and cotton and leave it outside her door. I whisper to the priest how I've heard her stories so often I have to cut her off midway to save my sanity. "This time she'll tell you how a nice young man broke her heart. But, Father, remember it's partly the medicine that confuses her. Everything's jumbled up in her head."

Entering the room, he notices the picture of the Sacred Heart of Jesus. Then Hedda starts in exactly as I said she would.

"I know the one who broke my heart," she says.

Her nightstand is filled with pills and water glasses. Gray curls fall out from her nightcap. She wears her glasses, and the counterpane is pulled up and tucked under her arm. Her rosary hangs from the bedpost.

"Hedda, Father Nowak is here."

We're already beside her when she answers, "Come in!" She reaches for the priest's hands. "You must know I wanted the baby, Father."

"Hedda!" I say. "Stop it. No more tall tales."

"Yes, Father. Now that you've seen an old lady in her nightcap, may I tell you something?"

"Go on," the priest says. So she proceeds with her favorite story.

"The river's name is 'Left-Handed.' A Left-Handed River. Do you know why we call it that?"

"Indians called it that," I say.

"Don't intrude, Julia," she says.

"But, Dear, I want to get you moving. Father Nowak doesn't have all morning," I say.

"Well, as they canoed in from Lake Superior, the Indians saw a river to the left. 'Nemadji' means 'Left-Handed.' Another Ojibwe word is 'Onawe.' It means 'Awake, Beloved.' Those are the two I know."

"In seminary, we studied Latin," the priest says.

"Hurry," I tell Hedda. "Let's get to the point."

"Well, I have a rather startling story," my sister says. "I hope you'll believe it on faith, Father, as you believe in the Trinity on faith. If you're willing to, then believe me when I say that my dead child returned once—from the dead, I tell you—and even muttered in his sleep when he opened his eyes a minute. He was a wonderful, silent, sleeping child whose dreams no doubt were pleasant for him. Are you able to believe that human beings return after death to us and sometimes sleep in the world for months, even years?"

Father Nowak takes the chair by her bed. He doesn't seem the least startled by her story. Perhaps, then, his imagination is large enough to listen to what she will tell him, I think.

"This man who made me pregnant and broke my heart," Hedda says, "between us, there'd been certain difficulties. He was a stronger person than I. I found out about my weak heart where a sidewalk ends at the edge of town. That's where he told me he was married and had a nice house. He was always one-up on me, this man, this lover. 'I was sure you weren't a denier, a person to say no,' I told him when it was all over. 'But I guess your marriage complicated matters for us. Such pain does happen, I see.'"

"Yes, I've seen it," says the priest.

"Now that we're so intimate, Father, do you want to know more disappointments I've suffered through, more crises of faith? It's easy to understand how they've occurred. Where was the confessor to hear what I'd done? My faith had deserted me. I was very much alone, so what could I do in turn but abandon my God?" She points to the picture of the Sacred Heart. "For me, it was either faith in Him or earthly love, and I chose what I needed at the moment. It was Christ's heart or mine on earth that I had to keep from breaking."

Now I bother my sister to interrupt her. "Take your pill. Here's water." She takes the pill from my hand, sips the water. "Too many pills!" she says.

Outside, the city buses roar down West Third Street; in the distance, horns and sirens blare. The bright, dry morning is perfect for early spring. Everywhere children outdoors will be happy, I think. In the school yard across the street, they laugh and run about. The Sisters of St. Joseph of the Third Order of St. Francis have them singing Easter songs a month early, songs which drift in through the window with the sun.

The priest helps Hedda put down her glass. He smoothes her pillow, guides her head back. "You know," he says, "life's big events are pretty easily counted, I've come to see: four or five passionate moments to mark the years. I count my First Communion, Ordination, and first Mass, my mother's death and two or three other important events as the sum of my life. Perhaps they've been fewer for you, but just as important. Is there anything else you must tell me?"

"No, Father."

"Then, Hedda, having heard your confession, that you have experienced a loss of faith, I want to say to you in Latin, *Ego te absolvo . . .* Go and sin no more."

"Don't absolve me of anything yet, Father," she says. "The child lived in my womb fifteen weeks. Do you understand? The baby disappeared before it was born. Don't look for it out there on the playground. I have for years. My lover sat in the waiting room of a hotel, then excused himself to buy some winter pants. When he returned it was over. The baby was gone. 'You could've sat with me,' I said. He unwrapped the new pants.

"In another hotel, a little more expensive one, I lay awake. He stayed a day on business, then went home to try on the pants again. Left to myself, I stared at the ceiling. It was raining outside. I guessed it would for a month. Now it had started raining through the ceiling. I lay on the bed in the rain which came in around the ceiling light, then spread to the corners until, finally, the whole ceiling was raining. But I rested. I was not so weak the morning after the loss of my child, but I was sick and worried over what I'd done. That was the start of my incompleteness. The rain stopped but the thunder didn't. I lay in the wet room thinking. And where was he but home in his new pants as I lowered myself into the bathtub which had those claw feet on it. As I dreamt of my child in this mean hotel, I wept. Taking the train home, I made it in time for work the next day.

" 'You were crazy to think it'd work out. It was impractical,' he said when we met again.

" 'Angelo, Angelo,' I said, 'how often you deceived me.' "

That happened to Hedda forty years ago, I think.

"Father, I do what I can to keep Hedda's room fresh," I say. "In warm weather, I keep the windows open, though not too much. The sound of children hurts her. She takes Inderal for her heart. Sometimes she has breathing problems. I used to keep fresh flowers in the room, didn't I, but they bothered your breathing, Hedda, didn't they? Ten years is a long time to live in one room and not move about the house, so I do what I can for her, Father. I bring up the radio or change the lampshade for day or evening use. She prefers the rose-colored one at night. I also keep her water glass full. This room, you'll see, has plain wallpaper. Sometimes I think patterned paper would give her more to look at."

I don't know how we've spent the hours, I think, but it's suddenly close to noon. We've all been sitting here, dreaming, Hedda staring at the ceiling. The alarm clock's ticking must have softened the morning sadness, calming us all.

"Has she told you the story of the odd, wandering family?" I ask.

"No," Father says.

"I want to make sure she doesn't repeat herself the way she does with me."

"Please feel free to go on," Father Nowak says.

"Well, let me begin for her," I say. "It's startling, a truly startling coincidence, but that very same week she lost her baby in the hotel room, another child came into her life. You'll never believe this, Father. It will take great faith to believe it. He was a member of a pious family of travelers who bowed their heads before they ate," I tell him. "Hedda has told me so often how they'd taken a table at the place where she worked during the trouble in her life. She was a waitress at the Lake Shore Cafe. Until the boy dropped a piece of bread or a biscuit from the table, the family had been eating quietly with no problems. Then came a stir. 'You know better,' the man beside him said. Hedda and I presume it was the boy's father. Anyway, he slapped the child's wrist. The boy forgot to kiss the bread he'd picked up from the floor. This must have been the family's custom. You could see they were tired, Hedda has always said, and that the man did not slap him in anger.

The child cried, then fell asleep on the man's shoulder. They were all so tired from traveling, I think."

"That boy renewed himself," Hedda breaks in. "If you could've seen it, the love between them all . . . how without fear he put his head on his father's shoulder, even though the father had corrected his behavior. The child knew where affection could be expected to come from. You could never count on me like that," Hedda says. Pulling back the curtain, she gazes out the window. "All of them but the boy got up when they were done. He rested his head against the back of the chair and slept. I whispered, 'Awake, Beloved.' I couldn't look at him long, for I had to work in the kitchen. When I returned and he was there, it dawned on me—"

"Father Nowak, they'd paid and left," I say.

"Walked out on their son?"

"Yes, certainly," says Hedda. She seems to be gathering strength from recalling it. "And he was a fine boy, Father. His hair was soft and brown. White down appeared at his temples. Though his face looked as if he'd known the world many years, there was nothing harsh about it. His lips were so smooth. His wise head bent forward like my own child's would have been if he was alive in me. Those rainy days—what had I done? It was hard believing my own baby had gone away. And now this . . . Give me my pills, Julia!"

I do, Theolair, which she must take several times a day. Her difficulty breathing causes her heart to swell. Her poor heart works hard, the doctors say. To them everything's physical. But how do we know it's not bursting for other reasons?

The pill settled, she breathes normally again. She clears her throat, looks at the priest. "My losses grip me," she says. "Except for Julia, I have been alone for forty years. Just me, Julia, and the Trinity, a different Trinity from the one you worship, I'm afraid, Father. That evening the sleeping child was abandoned I had to return to the kitchen. The other waitresses and some of the cooks huddled around him. Customers came by and gawked. As he slept, some of them touched his hands or his hair. It'd begun raining. Where was his family? I wondered. Could they have left one so helpless, so simple and helpless? Was my own unborn child dreaming of me in his loneliness? Was it coincidence they'd come so soon apart? Was it God's design?"

"Stop a minute, Hedda," I tell her. "It was Christian of her to look after him so well while he was there in the restaurant, wasn't it, Father?"

"Yes, I think it was," the priest replies. "To abandon a child like that!"

"And the faith she exercised watching over this . . . sleeper, didn't it mitigate her own sin?"

"Perhaps."

"And you, Father, do you accept on faith that anyone could sleep this long?"

"Well, strange things happen in life, and we must have faith to find the truth of what is revealed to us. What harm is there believing somebody can sleep an hour or two in a restaurant? It's no question of spiritual faith."

"But that's just it! She says it was a *year*, not an hour he slept alone."

"It puzzles me that here memory fails when I can remember all else," Hedda says. "He came so soon after my loss—that's maybe why I'm so confused about him, whether he stayed an hour, half a year, a year."

"It's okay," I say, trying to calm her. I look at the priest. But Hedda starts in again. "Yes, perhaps winter and spring were short . . . and summer never came, and there was no fall. Say that year you could count autumn weather in minutes, then the snow fell. An hour, a year, what difference? Maybe to me a year was like an hour that time. You know how, when you look back, sometimes your entire life seems to have been no longer than a few ill-chosen moments. Well, why not this? Why couldn't this happen?" Hedda asks.

She pauses a minute as if to collect her thoughts.

"They'd left him to my care," she says. "They'd extended their goodness by trusting someone who looked as though she'd allow no harm to visit a sleeping child. Do you see the irony? The boss of course thought it was great. His business doubled. People were coming in to eat and look at the sleeping boy in the chair. I would wipe his face with a damp cloth and sit beside him when I wasn't busy. The boss was good that way. After hours, I would try to hold the boy before I went home. Having looked after him when I could during the day, I'd go home long after midnight. I'd see his face looking out at me from cars parked in the rain. At home as I looked in the mirror, I'd see him over my shoulder in the corner of the room, just sitting sleeping with his head bowed. In my sleep I saw him crying. When his mother finally did return she made nothing special of all this. 'It's happened before,' I remember her saying. 'We hope he hasn't been trouble.' She threw her coat around the boy's shoulders and guided him out of the restaurant. 'We hope he hasn't been trouble . . .' That and nothing more and they were gone."

Hedda looks up, as if she hates to return from the comfort of dreams. Over the past forty years nothing has counted but her losses.

"So, Father, I set my clock to dream of resurrection—and withdrew. Though I continued to search the playground of St. Adalbert's School, nothing came of it. Thankfully, I didn't end up downstairs in the house. My heart couldn't take climbing up here to look out. I can see fine from here in this room." She points from her bed to the window and the children of St. Adalbert's playing below on this sunny day in spring. "I keep looking for my son."

"It's important for her to look out," I say.

"You know," she says, "the town suits me fine. East-side streets are named West Third or West Cedar. Our street is. When they founded the town, the roads laid down a half-mile from the first houses were west-side streets. But the town expanded from its origins, so what is now the east-side has old, west-side street numbers in place. How things pass me by, Father Nowak, how I'm stuck here on West Third.

Forty years I've worshipped the wrong Trinity, a baby fifteen weeks in my womb, a sleeping boy of about twelve or thirteen, and I, Hedda Borski, a recluse now dying, who almost gave birth. I was the third member of my Trinity."

She is quiet a moment. At such times, the alarm's ticking seems louder than ever.

"There's talk of straightening the river," she says suddenly. "Next fall they'll straighten and lengthen it, making it a Right-Handed River, if you can imagine that. To do so, they'll bring a bulldozer and barge upriver, then dredge a course for the river through the island into the bay."

"West-side streets are becoming east-side streets, too," says the priest to console her. "Everything is getting restored to how it was. We're expecting new days."

She looks around at us, at the sunlight on the curtain, at the painting on the wall. Our Blessed Jesus points to His heart, a very sacred heart. Much too big to be contained in His bosom, it rises outside of His body in flames.

"No, he wasn't. No trouble at all," she begins again. "Quiet. Never troublesome, my child slept, dreamt the whole time with head bent forward, the wise look on his face. Such a baby you've never seen. I fed him, carried him in the rain, left him in the city. The sleeper, too. I remember the boy. If I set the clock on the bureau, Father, it'll be my time before long. I've lived long enough. I want to join God's Holy Trinity. Let me think that I was no denier and that somewhere that sleeping boy naps in a chair in the afternoon sun. Allow me to dream that my poor, sleeping son is still coming back the first hour I hear steam shovels down by the river. Please, dear God, allow me the deceptions I can summon now that I have faith."

"*Ego te absolvo*," the priest says again. He whispers to me, "Even if she is wrong, do you condemn the heart's last stirrings, Julia?"

"It's raining," Hedda says. She's sighing.

"Hurry," Father says, "light the candles." Then I know. He begins his prayers. In the hall, I have the bread and salt, the six balls of cotton to anoint her with.

"Confiteor Deo omnipotenti . . ."

She joins him, "I confess to Almighty God, to Blessed Mary, ever Virgin, to Blessed Michael the Archangel, to Blessed John the Baptist, to the Holy Apostles Peter and Paul, and to all the Saints, that I have sinned exceedingly in thought, word and deed . . ."

"Mea culpa, mea culpa, mea maxima culpa," he says as he strikes his breast. *"Idea precor beatam Mariam semper Virginem . . ."*

She follows him, "I beseech Blessed Mary, ever Virgin, Blessed Michael the Archangel, Blessed John the Baptist, the Holy Apostles Peter and Paul, and all the Saints, and you, Father, to pray for me."

"May Almighty God have mercy on you, forgive you your sins, and bring you to life everlasting," he says. But she does not answer.

"My unborn child," she says after a moment. She tries taking the priest's hands. "Don't forget my baby of fifteen weeks. I won't leave him again."

But out on the playground, children's shrieks of joy drown her out, and we can't hear. They're so happy it's nice out.

"It makes the ceiling wet, the rain," Hedda says louder, as though frantic now to speak. "Don't leave him out there."

She seems to struggle with the rain we can't see. Across Third Street, the Sisters of St. Adalbert's School ring the school bell. Children's voices pour in through the window with the sunlight. They are going into the building for the last time in Hedda's life.

"He's drowning!"

Father uncovers her hands and feet. Then we hurry to bring in the table with the white linen cloth and accessories. He will give her Last Rites. I stop a moment to adore the Sacred Heart. It bursts from Christ's garments, a heart too large for Its body and all in flames. He is showing It to us. What is Its message? What fits the heart's wanting?

I can't make out what It is saying to us. When I look again, Hedda's gone. Her head has slipped forward to her chest, eyes gazing nowhere if not at her own broken heart. Perhaps now she has gone to join the sleeper and her very own son. I think how it doesn't matter if I close her eyes to the sunlight.

"Blessed is the Holy Trinity and undivided Unity," Father Nowak is saying. He stands riffling through the pages of his book for appropriate prayers. He cannot seem to give it up and prays well on toward three o'clock as though embarrassed about sending her away in the rain.

The Korporał's Polonaise

Looking one last time at the Polish Eagle painted on the bow of the freighter *Pomorze Zachodnie,* we cursed the captain and scrambled down the gangway. That November day Mr. Lasinski, who worked at the flour mill in the East End of Superior, never thought he'd be taking home a family of sailors along with the cartons of *Żywiec* beer he'd gone to the docks to buy from the crew.

After the newspaper articles, television reports, and INS interviews, a few months later as we clean palms in the church basement, we recall it all again for him, our sponsor. For a moment I think of the priest upstairs in the sanctuary. We fear St. Adalbert's Church will close like the other churches. Frightened of this, in confession later I will tell the priest why I left the Old Country. He will tell me his own fears for the *new* country.

"Bless me, Father," I will say.

"What are your sins, Kazimierz Wroblewski?"

"Despair, Father."

"I despair, too," he will say. "We're both desperate."

Every Sunday since I've been here the priest has carried his grief and mine to the altar. Tomorrow here and in the Old Country priests wear red vestments during the Mass and distribution of palms. Tomorrow Marcella Dzikonski will play the organ in Superior, Wisconsin, the way my father did for many years in the Church of St. Bartholomew in Poland.

Mr. Lasinski calls our story "immigrant history," saying we should record it for future generations like Tomasz, my son's. "Will you tell more?" asks Stanislaus Lasinski when my thoughts return to what I was saying about a merchant seaman's life.

I tell him how, in Poland, my father will attend Palm Sunday Mass; how later, tucking the palm behind the portrait of my mother on the wall of the room, he'll dream of her, then of me, Kazimierz, of Hedwig my wife, and of young Tomasz all come to the Seaway Port of Superior. "When I was very young, my own father carried me through the village like I once did my Tomaszu. 'Precious Kazik,' he called me. He kept me close to his heart," I tell Mr. Lasinski. "My father was organist at the church when I was small. '*Pan* Organist . . . Sir Organist,' people called him. This was in 'the Land of Graves and Crosses.' This was my Poland. *To był moja Polska.*"

"This is the Poland you left with Hedwig, who was cook on the *Pomorze Zachodnie*, and with your Tomasz?"

"Yes. Life is no good where we came from. The Communists. Speak against them and you're a 'dwarf of reaction . . . *karzeł reakcji.*' 'Social noxiousness . . . *społeczna szkodliwość,*' they call it. For years we dreamt of coming here. The northeast wind brought us."

Hedwig looks out the church's basement window at our nine-year-old Tomasz playing in the school yard. Her eyes brighten. We need such joy before I tell how we've abandoned my father. *I wish I could send these remarks to you in Poland, dear Father, so you could hear me recall your death and resurrection. Now you must stop to rest your elbows on the table you are so weary. When you roll your sleeves, your arms, I imagine, will be thinner than when I last saw you. My only hope is your dear smile so far away in Passion Time. How I miss you and regret leaving.*

*What could I do? I have my wife, my boy. When you yourself once left me,
can you now call your son, Kazimierz, "cygan . . . gypsy," for leading his
family to America?*

Hedwig, who's been patiently cleaning the palms' silk threads and
listening, says, "When a musician passed through during the war, he'd
come to Kazimierz's house just as a visiting priest would look up a priest
in the village or a teacher, a teacher, a butcher, a butcher. Wanderers
knew who lived where."

"I was very young, our Tomasz's age, when my father left. He
joined the Home Army. Overrun, Poland fought back in 1939. *'Ojciec,*
Father,' I remember crying, asking him not to leave."

Now as I think of him, the silence moves rapidly. What have I
done? When my dear father is at some distance from the son Kazimierz's heart, I begin again, more composed. "After he put me to bed,
saying he'd see me in the morning, *Pan* Organist ducked into the
forests. 'Where is Father?' I asked Grandfather when the sun rose.

"'Gathering mushrooms,' he said.

"'When will he return?'"

"If you only knew, Mr. Lasinski!" says Hedwig. "The Russian filth
watched us then and now in 1985. Think of the Katyn Forest Mas-
sacre, think of 'the Flower of Polish Youth' slaughtered there in World
War Two by the Russians. The heart yearns for them, Mr. Lasinski.
And God help us what the Nazis did to Poland and the Jews."

"Now Father had gone," I tell our sponsor from the flour mill. "I
looked for him by the woodpile, by the pools where leaves swirled
above the fish, by the church where no one practiced *'Bogurodzica.'*
Occasionally you'd hear whispered, 'An organist has come! An organist
has come!' The first time I ran so hard to the fields near home I stumbled over the wagon ruts but got up and kept on. It was the pattern I
followed many times during the war. Scanning the roads, going farther
each time, I muttered, 'Where is my father? Has he deserted us? Why
can't he stay and protect me?'

"When Father left, the house was silent. He's not praying for us. He's gone, I'd begun to think."

"How sad it sounds now," Hedwig says. She's washed kneelers, dusted windows, washed the church floor today. For Hedwig, who left only a cousin and a distant uncle in Poland, it may be a little easier forgetting the voyage. Nothing keeps me from remembering Father today, however. The thought of the vigil lamp on the altar of St. Bartholomew's in our village in the Old Country—Christ's heart at the center of His church—keeps me remembering.

"What our country has suffered," says Hedwig. "Go on telling it."

"Rumors circulate," I say. "They swirl about the eaves, sweep down through the chimney. I remember how hard Grandmother *Babusia* prayed when the rumor came to our door that Father had died. Mother fell to her knees. People had heard it on roads, under trees, through open windows. In the late afternoon, I ran off. The priest came looking for me. An Old Country priest, he feared the devil and the forest. 'Think of your mother and grandmother,' he said, summoning his courage. He was old like the priest upstairs today. He'd borrowed Pomerinski's horse to come to get me. 'You must return home, Kazimierz,' he said, 'not stay in these woods. You can't run away from truth.'

" 'I'm waiting for Father.'

" 'What shelter do you have?' asked the priest. 'You'll get cold. I don't want to be like the moon bringing trouble to your hearth. Come here tomorrow morning, but for now, please Kazimierz, I am old. I don't want to stay. Come now, please take the reins. I fear for our souls in these woods.'

"Mother rekindled the fire when we came home. 'Are you sure about the rumor?' asked the priest. 'Look in the ashes!' Grandfather said.

"For months the priest told me, 'We must serve out God's design. Don't give up.' So I ran to the fields with hope and conviction. 'Have you seen Father? Please,' I asked wanderers, 'have you word? He is as tall as you and strong. This *korporał* would be talking about playing the

organ at the Church of St. Bartholomew. I am his Kazimierz. Did you
see the man whose eyes are said to resemble mine? Why have we not
heard from the *korporał?*'

"Once I thought we had news. A fearsome-looking Russian whose
black eyebrows matched his eyes swore he'd tell me if I sang him
'Vlanka, the Heartbreaker.' He said it *'Vlanka Kliuchnik'* in Russian.
When I sang, he said he must have another song. I said I didn't know
another Russian song. 'I can't tell you my news then,' he said, laughing,
walking off through the fields.

"Another time a man selling trapped souls came by. The souls
weren't very heavy, but he was loaded down with them. They hung
from his shoulders and belt in little boxes. Animals' souls, Russians'
souls, everyone's souls. 'Get away. I don't want them loose on earth!' he
said when I ran up.

"'Do you have Father? Where are you going to put him?'

"'I'll bury him, sell him, place him in a tree. On windy nights, the
box will sing to the tree:

> Hi! Ho! Hi!
> What a man am I!
> Hi! Ho! Hi!
> A valiant man am I!

"'Please can I see my poor father's soul so I may buy it from you
for three or four *złoty?*'

"'You carry the box. Do no more than that. No peeking inside!'

"The man grunted. Sometimes he spit at my feet. His hair and face
were greasy, it looked like, with the grease of Russian engines and
motors and coal. This box was made of willow switches, clay, paste,
string. I thought if I could free Father maybe war would end. When we
got to the village, the man cursed me when I gave him the three-*złoty*
reward for rescuing Father. 'There's a dog's soul, nothing else, in that

one, foolish boy. All the miles you've sung to a dog's soul and now paid me for it. I even know its name, *Kurta* the Dog. I've tricked you. Hi! Ho! Hi! What a man am I! Here *Kurta*! Here, Boy,' he called and whistled for the soul of a dog.

"The priest watched me, crying, hang the empty box in a tree to listen for songs from the *korporal* when the wind blew. It was a silent country, though. The soul was gone.

"As ashes are swept from a hearth, so after a while was my father's memory swept from the village. No one spoke of the *korporal* anymore. I wondered each day, has Father sent a rumor through the wind only to make it look as though he's died? Is he buying a widow a loaf of Russian bread or a wick for her lamp? I shall not pray for him, I decided. Let the rumor go back that we're not praying for Father whose kiss means nothing. The *korporal's* embrace can mean nothing ever again.

" 'Bless me, I have sinned,' I confess over and over to another 'father,' the priest, in the Port of Superior. I've confessed here and at a church in Duluth. *How can I have thought so of my father and at that age given my soul to despair? In what past or future am I? I wonder.*

" 'Have you other sins?' ask the priests.

" 'Despair, sorrow, anger. We *had* to leave the ship. For Poles, a seaman's life is not so bad under Communist regime, but nothing is as good as being in your country in this northern port.'

"Then the priests ask, 'What other sins must you confess, Kazimierz Wroblewski, merchant seaman? Hurry before churches *all* close.'

" 'Despair, loneliness. We can't go back to him.'

" 'Hurry! Hurry, our closing is imminent.'

"Over and over I tell the priests that Hedwig and I are the rumors of despair. Is our voyage worthy of retelling? Is it, when tomorrow my father will go to Mass alone thinking of Mother who died long ago, then thinking of the family that went to America? People will ask him after church, 'When will your Kazimierz return?' Later, he'll place the lunch bowl on the cloth, lie in bed, look out the window at the agent watching the house. I have such images of a beloved father—white hair brushed back, thin, white eyebrows over eyes closed on nearly a century of struggle, nose curved at the bridge, white moustaches. Now he must doubt me, his middle-aged son, and ask the Crucifix and the ashes in the hearth, 'Where has Kazimierz gone with his soul? On what sea is his soul tonight?'

"By midsummer, Mr. Lasinski, I'd tell Mother, 'I won't be out long tonight.'

" 'So the news, is it good news on the roads you walk looking for your father?'

" 'No, Mother,' I'd say, disappointing her. 'No souls, though I sat with the trap open.' *This is the night she, too, will leave us, I'd think. What will happen to me?* As the candle flickered, Mother would open the latch door and, in the starlight, sweep leaves from the doorstep.

" 'Why are you sweeping?' I'd ask.

" 'Couldn't sleep. The news, Kazimierz?'

" 'No good news, Mother.'

"What I learned I kept to myself. I'd hang the box in a tree at night. Soon I gave up believing I could trap my father's soul; and the twine that tied the willow switches broke on the box and the paste and glue gave way on the box that trapped no soul.

"Now autumn and winter passed, and the long, cool spring of 1944 had begun when one day, walking to *Pani* Grotnik's, I saw two young sisters running toward me. 'An organist . . . !' they cried. When they grabbed my sleeve and insisted, 'Kazimierz, a rider saw him!', I paid no attention.

"They were twelve years old. One of them had scuffed her knee. They went running to neighbors' houses.

" 'Who?' people called.

" 'Out on the post road. Everyone come!' Zosia and Marta were saying. 'An organist.'

"I'd run to the roads one hundred times. Now in the mist I saw someone. As Zosia and her sister ran, I dawdled, observing the pools of rain in the wagon tracks, the clumps of grass. What excitement could compel me to run? When I looked back, there stood Grandfather at the cottage door.

"The priest trotting past on Pomerinski's horse was calling, '*Zprochu powstałeś i w proch się obrócisz . . .* Dust thou art and to dust thou shalt return.' The distant figure . . . there one minute, in the next he'd be lost in the meadow blackthorns.

"How could a man be so haggard-looking? I wondered when he drew closer.

" 'Grimy fellow!' one of the village women said.

"His coat trailed around him in the mud. I wondered whether this stranger would ask for 'Vlanka the Heartbreaker.' "

"War casts up odd, frightening people. Ghosts," Hedwig says.

"I'd come to hate the rags and filth of beggars—the embarrassment I suffered when they passed through. Zosia, her sister, the priest on horseback, the villagers; we kept watching this man stumble closer. Stopping a moment to adjust the rags he'd wound around his neck, he caught his breath, observed the millet fields, the old people who'd come out to see him. Christ has come, they said. But it was no Christ they wanted. They'd been cheated.

" 'Tell me of *Korporał* Wroblewski,' I said. 'I'll show you a box. I'll sing you an Easter song.'

" 'A ghost!' said Zosia.

" 'Do you know my father? Where is *Korporał* Wroblewski?' I asked.

" 'Stand away,' said the priest, who started praying.

" 'No one knows your father,' the man said. 'No one knows *Korporał* Wroblewski, who's dead.'

" 'Does the devil not know *Korporał* Wroblewski?' asked the priest.

" 'Yes, the devil,' said the man. 'The devil and I know him!'

"The women wiped their tears. '*Jesu,* no one even recognizes the devil anymore!'

"'Hi! Ho! Hi! A valiant man am I,' I sang, preparing to return home. 'I know him. It's a trick. He'll ask for something, three *złoty,* then tell you nothing. *Nie ma Ojca.* I have no father.'

"Beneath the dirt where the wanderer's skin had peeled, the new skin was white on his face. The dirt caked most of his forehead and cheeks. You could hardly see his eyes. Sometimes his lips moved . . . no sound came out. Bits of rags stuck to his hands—his fingers like crow's claws. 'I can go no further,' he said.

"'*Nie ma Ojca.* What a valiant man am I without a father,' I said. Imitating the slump of the man's shoulders, I circled him, repeated a rhyme from the old children's game *Raz, Dwa, Trzy:*

> One, two, three,
> The devil's watching, see?
> Four five, six,
> Watch out for his tricks.

'Another demon,' I said and struck him, struck the devil.

"*Babusia* was crying. 'O *Boże.* Not dead.' I saw her making the sign of the cross. The priest, too, was whispering 'Christ!' Whoever it was, I'd been embarrassed before by a man carrying a dog's soul and could not understand what this wanderer was whispering to us.

"But the villagers now started saying it. 'It is the *Korporał Organista.*' Ha! *I* know the devil, I thought. No father leaves his son. The tricks this demon uses. I had learned so much in the fields, you see, Mr. Lasinski, that now *my* soul was trapped. You could write 'ANGER. SELFISHNESS. PRIDE' on the box that held my soul. I have brought it to America. It is small enough to hold in the hand. I was a precious, selfish boy. I would not even recognize him that day or all during Holy Week, which now years later we celebrate in a free country where my soul is trapped in new delusions to help me forget.

"The whole week of his passion and resurrection I denied him until, one day late in the month of March 1944, I saw him sitting alone resting in the sun. He'd gained strength. He was smoking his pipe, smiling about something. Nodding to me, he said, 'Aren't you happy I'm home, Kazimierz? My little Kazik, I have been defending our country. Come, sing me a Polonaise, hum the melody for your father.'

"He said it so softly, Mr. Lasinski. They were like the words of God. Hearing them I did as he said. He loved a Polonaise by Count Ogiński. 'La-la-la-la-la,' I sang it. I could see tears form in his eyes. Wiping them back for him, I went in the house then and buried myself in his coat whose buttons I kissed for many years afterward." *How selfish a youth I was in Poland, Dearest Father Korporał. Forgive me. Sometimes I have the hope that I can sing for you an Easter song and we will be together, then I know it's too late.*

"But this box! Hedwig, can you bring it to us, the box from the Old Country, the box with the Polonaise? Its delicate mechanism will play it."

"I'll get the music box upstairs, Kazimierz."

"Tomorrow the palms my father tucks behind Mother's and Grandmother's portraits will wither, Mr. Lasinski. Look at the palms in our church basement. Their scent reminds me of fields I ran through when Father returned. Then to come home to see his son bewitched and turned against him. And to hear how his son thought he'd captured a soul! Today in March 1985 the lamp in the sanctuary burns; the Pascal Candle is in its place in back of the church; and *Korporał Organista* has come home to me again in my tale of Passion Week. I could not tell him to his face that we were planning to leave him last autumn. If I did, the despair would have been so great I could not have lived. The thought of my father, the *korporał*, alone today . . . Hedwig, bring the box! Play Ogiński's 'Farewell to My Country.'"

"I'm coming, Kazimierz. Patience."

"Raz, Dwa, Trzy!" my son's voice interrupts me. He is teaching others the "One, Two, Three" rhyme.

"Look, there's your Tomasz," says Mr. Lasinski.

In he walks just as I am finishing my story.

"Tomasz, son," says Hedwig. "Where have you been? Sing us *Raz, Dwa, Trzy.*"

My boy's hair is tousled from the wind, his face windburned. He is excited, happy. He's made friends at St. Adalbert's Polish grade school at Twenty-Third Avenue East and East Third Street in the Seaway Port of Superior. Let me have time with him before he too must grow up and leave.

"Would you like to say something, Tomasz?" Mr. Lasinski asks. "We'd like to hear *your* opinion on matters."

He catches us by surprise. Out of breath, my Tomasz says, "I don't want to return to Poland. I want to stay in America."

"So do I, Tomaszu," I say, a merchant seaman from a village where my father waits alone praying for our return. "I don't want to either. There's nothing there but graves and crosses."

Now Hedwig, coming downstairs with a little box of music for trapped souls, says it. "There's nothing to go home for."

Above us, in a church that is to close, the despairing priest prepares for his last Palm Sunday as I open the music box on the table and find a lock of my father's precious white hair. Now the Polonaise he loved begins to play, but we cannot go back to him. We cannot return to the Old Country. All we have are graves and crosses.

The Tools Of Ignorance

1.

THE VOICES I HEARD

I wipe beer glasses at the bar of Heartbreak Hotel in Superior. I turn the radio dial. I wonder where do the short, sweet years go to? Last season I got free drinks and Shrimp-Busters at Herby K's, got my muffler fixed free at Mufflers of Shreveport, got autograph requests all up and down Louisiana Avenue. That's before the bartender at Herby K's and the waiters at the Hayride Kitchen in Shreveport turned their backs on me. It is a story of loss and regret that has brought me home to Wisconsin.

Now who do I have to listen to but Pete Katzmarck in the corner of the bar staring at the hands of the Hamm's Beer clock? I tell him, "You're pickled. Go on home, you gaboosh, Pete."

"*You* go home, Augie," Pete says to me. "If I cou'n't hit no better'n you, I'd never sign a contract. Bitter, bitter disappointment, *gorzki*."

"*Starosc nieradość*," this other old guy, Wladziu, moans in Polish. "Old age ain't any fun."

Somebody plugs in the jukebox, Eddie Blazonczyk's band comes on. Horns and accordions begin. On the phonograph record a guy yells:

Polka Time! Polka Time!
We're all fine at Polka Time!

I turn down the baseball game playing on the radio. Since it is growing dark, I flick on the switch to light the outdoor sign. Even the blue neon is heartbroken. Sizzling a little, only parts come on: HEARTBREAK   OTEL.

I look in the mirror back of the bar. Everywhere I see myself. Behind the bottle of *Jeżynowka* blackberry it's me Augie, barkeep. Bum. Loser. I see me in Pete's face . . . in the old guys' faces slobbering over bowls of beer. Losers. Derelicts. Gabooshes.

"*You* go home!" Pete says.

"I've got nothing there but my ma waiting, Petie. What'll I do at home? I'm better off here. Either way I'm washed up. Jeezus, I threw my life away. I should've married this gal I knew down in Shreveport. What do I got now when I can't do nothing but think about her? I'm twenty-five. I'm through. No more baseball except what I play to embarrass myself on Sundays."

"You look like shit on Sundays," someone calls from the other end of the bar.

Over the cloudy jar of pickled pigs' feet, I stare in the mirror, wishing a storm would come to steam up the mirror and blow out the neon sign in front so I could serve the guys by flashlight or candlelight. Then you couldn't see our ceiling that's turned orange from seventy years of smoke or the mirror or the nicks in the long wood bar.

I've got to get a better job, or someday I'll be a washed-up geezer taking Pete's spot at the bar. I can't get over Shreveport, though. My heart's in Shreveport on the Red River because of what happened. Was it the night we returned from Jackson and Ellie Pleasaunt was waiting at the players' entrance to the stadium? Somehow I got tangled up in something very serious in Shreveport that was partly the result of my foolishness and pride and partly my disregarding someone who loved me. It eats at me every night, so that when I look in the mirror behind the bar now and ask myself (above the polkas and schottisches), "Did you *really* love her?", the answer is still "yes" from my broken heart up north in the Yankeeland of Superior, Wisconsin.

Why I didn't listen to the Voice of the Shreveport Captains and keep from coming back to such a miserable place of heartbreak as the East End is a two-year history of bus trips, doubleheaders, and rain delays. In this, Augie Wyzinski's true-life chronicle of lost love, I'll get the record-book stuff over first. Like how in high school I lined a "blue darter" into the screen that protects the windows of a paper mill in Menasha, Wisconsin—430 feet into a wind off Lake Winnebago. Like how after the Oshkosh game in college, with the season I had my junior year, the Giants signed me. The *Evening Telegram* of my hometown here had on its front page: "LOCAL BOY SIGNS." My ma, Uncle Louie, and I couldn't finish our dinner at The Polish Hearth for all the commotion. The Duluth paper wanted an interview, too. Bennett Stodill, the sports editor, wouldn't let me touch my cabbage rolls. "You're going to make it. I know that," he said. My ma smiled, my uncle patted my shoulder. "See?" Ma said as the future lit up for me.

The Giants assigned me to Clinton, Iowa. I tore up the league—Cedar Rapids, Kane County, Burlington. Ma sent clippings: "FUTURE BRIGHT FOR SIGNEE WYZINSKI" . . . "BIG CLUB TO PROMOTE LOCAL TO AA AFTER FULL SEASON IN IOWA. FRISCO NEXT?"

I wasn't going to toil in the low minors long, I told myself.

From Clinton the next season I went to Shreveport, Double-A. The first month there, April, I hit six homers, four doubles. After I tossed out my fifteenth base runner trying to steal, I couldn't walk into a clothing store or nightclub on Louisiana Avenue without someone buying me a shirt or a drink just so they could be near me. You've heard of such phenoms as me.

Everything was great. ("Everytink great," the old gabooshes would say.) Things like this happen. Guys get lucky. I come out of college, I come out of northern Wisconsin. At the right moment, success and love strike me. Maybe no one from here will ever again catch on like this. Uncle Louie would talk about a "Hurricane" Bob Hazle that rose out of nowhere late one season in the '50s to help the Milwaukee Braves win a pennant. Then he was gone into oblivion like me. Now I'll explain how *I*, Augie, oblivious Augie, ended up at Heartbreak Hotel where "the bellhop's tears keep flowin'" and show why *I*, Augie, forgotten Augie, wear a baggy wool uniform these days on Sundays in Superior instead of the one with the orange and black ^{S}F of the big club, San Francisco. This is where the voice I should have listened to comes in. There were fifty thousand watts of power behind that voice.

2.

GIANTS' SIGNEE ADVERTISES
GOODY'S HEADACHE POWDERS

Who'd argue with fifty thousand watts or question Biff Barton, the radio Voice of the Shreveport Captains? Mr. Barton had a full head of black hair he used Vitalis in. But in front it was like you could see each individual strand where it grew out of a really white scalp. His forehead and face were tanned. He wore tinted glasses that turned darker if the room or the press box was dark. Who'd argue with the power of that God-like voice? "Howdy, Louuu-eee-siana," he'd say over the airwaves with fifty thousand watts to back him up.

He studied us, studied statistics, talked about us. "You know," Mr. Barton would say when I saw him at Shooter's Smokehouse Cafe in Shreveport, "it's a great game I hope you stick with, kid." I knew he had faith in me. He interviewed me on the field after a Tulsa game. "Those were king-size homers last night," he said. "Your throwing arm is a rifle, too."

"I'm seeing the ball good, Mr. Barton," I said into the microphone as I looked into his dark glasses.

"I'll say it's early in the season. Kid, you don't know your strength. You're soon going to be living on the West Coast. Fans in the Ark-La-Tex listening to this broadcast: Come out-chere to have a look. He's liable to be gone soon."

"Keep your nose clean," he said to me afterward.

"Don't worry," I said. "No smoking. No drinking."

In Tulsa I threw out three more runners. I knocked in six runs in one game, five in another. In El Paso I hit a scorcher off the flagpole at Dudley Field. At Smith-Willis Stadium in Jackson, Miss., I got two doubles. Sportswriters called it a "meteoric" rise.

"Keeping my nose clean," I'd say when I saw Mr. Barton before games.

I kept on hitting and playing defense like the Milwaukee Braves' "Hurricane" Bob Hazle Uncle Louie told me about. June went by. "Everything was good then, wasn't it, Augie?" I ask myself in the mirror behind the bar now, recalling a four-for-four day game with San Antonio and the night that followed with Ellie, this woman who adored me. She was a lonely, lovesick fan. Before I met her I was out every night after games pulling hijinks at the Sports Page in Shreve Square, at Forrest and Lulu Longrie's Dugout Saloon on Line Ave., at The Cove on Cross Lake. So many women love a hard-hitting catcher that you can fill out different lineup cards every night. Once in a motel room after a twi-night doubleheader with Beaumont, a rookie named Denise, naked, wore my chest protector, crouched, and gave me a signal for a fast ball. Another time in my apartment after a tight home game with Midland, I wore the catcher's mask through the whole act of "coytis." But one moonlit night after gunning down four base runners and going two for three against the Arkansas Travelers, I got even luckier; I came home and pulled off a triple play with three gorgeous roommates who loved my swing. Then her, Ellie. She fell for me right away. We met at the Captains' Booster Club Pig Roast when I brought her a paper plate of coleslaw, pig meat, and Jo Jo's. Despite what sportswriters called my "furious pace," something was missing in my life and career like it was in Ellie's, I guess.

On the night I think of now, Ellie and I'd been going out a couple weeks. Her loneliness and the pressure on me of my sudden fame in the South, all of it—I don't know—came together that very night in the quiet of my apartment when we kissed each other's shoulders and hair. "I think I'm in 'like' with you," I told her, looking into the shadows of her face. You don't say such things to women on the first date. But it was three weeks we'd been dating, and I could honestly tell her I liked her and partially commit myself to her—except for when I felt the urge to go on the prowl, drinking and looking for women who appreciated my star quality.

"I'm deeply in 'like' with you, too, Augie," she said, looking up. "I'd give you my heart."

I buried myself in her neck and hair then.

The two of us lying there, I said her profile reminded me of a picture I'd seen of an ancient Egyptian queen, Never-Titty.

"I want you to feel like her husband," Ellie said.

"I wasn't alive back in ancient times before the designated hitter rule," I said.

"I was just teasing," she said. "I've been buried and you woke me and I'm in love. Nefertiti's in love." She moved a wisp of hair from her beautiful white forehead with the blue vein in her left temple. Like Never-Titty's, her nose had this very attractive bend. To me she was a goddess.

"We're not going to sleep this night," I said, "but I'm sure happy and don't give a darn. Lookit the homers I got today."

After all this baseball stardom, then Nefertiti giving me her heart, regret and misfortune had to follow. It just seems like whenever I'm on a roll I always do something dumb to mess things up. Maybe it's part of my personality that I don't know how to hold on to the good things. Maybe I got what's called "low self-esteem." Now I have come to be counseled by winos and gabooshes with a real high regard for themselves who, when I say "I ain't any good anymore," they say, "You're right."

"But I once was, wasn't I, boys?" I ask.

"You no good ever. You were lousy. You stunk. We seen you play in the old-timers' basebull league on Sunday, too. You stink."

But once not so long ago I was in Shreveport under blue Louisiana skies, and there I had a fine time and there I met a woman named Nefertiti. When I look in the mirror, I still see her, heartbroken, looking back. *When you said you'd give me your heart that night, Ellie, I looked in your eyes and said I would not hurt you, and later you carried my baby. On the night you gave me your love, I didn't know how much I would fail you. But I did fail you, Ellie Pleasaunt, because I could not accept your open, innocent love, because I did not have it in me.*

A month after the Tulsa interview I was Biff's guest again—this time when he was promoting Goody's at Winn-Dixie Grocery. "Anybody who's had a headache," Biff Barton said over 71 KEEL-Radio, "get down to Jewella Avenue. Meet the Voice of the Shreveport Captains and Biff's very special interview guest today." While Ellie called her ma to say, "Turn on KEEL, quick!", Biff had me practice what he'd written on a scrap of paper. "Catching's hard work," I was saying nervously over the airwaves before I knew it. "When I get home with sore muscles, what do I reach for?" Here Mr. Barton held out the microphone. "GOODY'S!" the customers in Aisle 7 shouted.

Every night last summer the Voice of the Shreveport Captains, the Old Testament God Biff Barton's voice, came over Big Thicket Country (as it does tonight when I am working in a bar in Superior a thousand miles away). You'd look up through the smoke haze in the late innings at Beaumont last year, see him in the little square lighted press box, see him at V. J. Keefe Stadium in San Antone, at Windham in Little Rock, looking down through his tinted glasses at the way we were carrying on. You'd pull into Marshall, Texas, and hear Mr. Biff, who influenced our manager's decisions. You might live on the bayou in Homer, Louisiana, or be up in Helena, Arkansas, fixing your car, and you'd hear Biff's scouting report and interview show from down on the field. *Did you pass Ellie Pleasaunt on your road trips, Mr. Barton? Did you see her crying when she learned we were going to have a baby?*

3.

TEXAS LEAGUE HOME RUN KING

My whole name is August Joseph Wyzinski. Old guys call me "Ow-goost." I was famous for a couple months, but I began wondering about my future when our manager, we called him the skipper, stopped looking me in the eye and benched me in Midland-Odessa in mid-July when I'd dropped a foul tip for strike three.

"Bet you'd go for a Polee Sausage," the skipper'd say and spit tobacco. Sometimes pronouncing it "Pulley sausage," he'd ask on the field, "What you Yankees up north call that stuff you eat?"

"Kielbasa."

"Well, from now on you're Augie Kielbasa with them sausage hands that cain't hold onto a baseball."

"Pete, you spilled your beer," I say a year later. Here's a bar rag. Wash your face while you're at it."

"You looking in mirror. What d'you know about my face?"

"I know. That's what I'm saying. I'll wipe *mine*, too."

Wipe my face with a bar rag because I have been a fool, Pete.

"Was I any good *ever* at anything, you guys?" I ask.

"No good. Right from the start, no good."

"Thanks."

"You welcome, Augie."

"Ah, who wants a bowl of beer on me? Why not play me for a fool? I've thrown it all away. But what's the use of telling you gabooshes? Just remind me I didn't deserve her and that I'm a fool. Tell me, Pete, was I a fool?"

"Sure, Augie."

"But why? I want to know."

"Because you are and you're no good with a baseball."

"Ah, you're right, Pete and you guys. That's what I don't understand about myself, how I can come so close to the good things and blow it every time. That's why I can't see any future for me. All I can do is think about the past. What kind of life is that to have?"

4.
"OW-GOOST'S" NIGHT OF TERROR
OR HOW "OW-GOOST" ALWAYS
MANAGES TO SCREW THINGS UP

One night last year we'd gone extra innings at home against the Beaumont Golden Gators, and though I hadn't caught, I was still tired. I'd been warming the bench, eating peanuts, thinking about my late nights with Ellie Pleasaunt and what I'd gotten into with her. I missed the night life—drinking, carousing, trading off of your fame to see how far you could get with a gal.

After Mr. Barton's stirring account of the game, KEEL-Radio had gone back to regular programming. Life was boring again. The parking lot was still burning from sixteen hours of Caddo Parish heat when all cleaned up I came out of the clubhouse with nowhere to go.

When you're famous and in a slump, you need something to cheer you up. You have a nice car from your signing bonus of a few years back and plenty of time after games. If you're short of dough, you fool gals who follow ballclubs by carrying a money clip with fifty bucks showing and a wad of one dollar bills beneath it. A few of the Captains have girl-friends in the Texas League towns. I had Ellie since I settled down from the wild days of April in Shreveport when I was out every night with Linda, D.J., Teri, and all the other women who came to watch me on the field and follow me off. Even so, I never promised Ellie Pleasaunt I'd be faithful. A star has a right to his fun.

Mostly, Ellie saw two or three games each homestand. When I hadn't seen her in the box seats, I thought she was home in Natchitoches with her folks. Sometimes after the game, she drove back the same night, sometimes stayed with her cousin Hattie in Shreveport, sometimes with me. I'd been to Cousin Hattie's with Ellie. She lived at The Knolls Apartments on Jesuit Avenue.

I'd once visited Ellie's folks in Natchitoches, too.

"Come in, Mr. Wyz—," Ellie's ma had said the first time I showed up.

"*Wyzinski*, Mother," Ellie'd said. "He's Polish."

"Praise the Lord, you're as handsome, Mr. Wyzinski, as Ellie said. Pardon me, I was just cleaning up around here. Mr. Pleasaunt will be home soon and we can all sit down to get acquainted. Come right in, son."

Good people, Christians, but love counts for something, too. When we were alone, Ellie'd get over her reservations about sin, and we would be together in the name of love and ancient Egypt, and she got pregnant.

* * *

This particular night, though, I needed time off from all the family stuff to figure how to get out of my slump. It was August. Things weren't so hot at the park. After a few times around the league, I'd stopped seeing the ball. My throws to second were off. Guys stole too easily on me. The skipper really started losing interest in me after my average dropped and my run production dried up because all the love and fame had jinxed me. If the weather didn't wear you down, then thinking of the women of April did. I figured maybe if I just got out on the town like I once did—meet some Louisiana gals, have some drinks—I'd be okay, get back my concentration, then settle in with the one who loved me.

Not ready for sleep, on this hot night I practiced my swing with the umbrella I'd gotten free at Hall Clothier and Bootery when I was the Prince of Louisiana Avenue. I was killing time in a parking lot swinging at bugs. I hit two moths for homers. "Dodgers' pitcher goes to the mound," I could imagine Vin Scully saying. "Wind blowing in tonight at venerable Candlestick Park. Wyzinski, the batter, steps in."

Around 11:30, with nothing to do, I pulled into a convenience store a thousand miles from the Heartbreak. "How you gals doin'?" I said to this lady and her friend running the place. Ready for some action I tried the money clip trick on them.

"Where *you* from?" one of them asked.

"Louisiana."

"You aren't with that funny accent," the other one said. Her name was "Honeydew." She was the store clerk. "You got 'America's Dairyland' license plates."

"I'm from Louisiconsin, a new state. Superior, Louisiconsin."

"I'm gonna stock the coolers, Joyce hon," Honeydew said, rolling her eyes.

"I'll have a Yoo-Hoo," I said.

Joyce rang one up the way I now ring up Stashu's vodka or Wladziu's blackberry brandy at the Heartbreak.

"My name's Race Gentry," I told her.

Honeydew came out to check on us.

"How you doing?" she asked.

"He wants to know how old I am. I rang up his Yoo-Hoo."

"You're twenty-seven, aren't you, Joyce?" asked Honeydew.

"Well how about making me an old lady. I swan, I'm not a day over twenty-six."

"I'd a guessed that," I said. "You look great to me."

Joyce wore these plastic shoes, just strips of white plastic. She had tan legs with little bumps in the skin around back of her thighs.

"Oh these?" she said when she noticed me looking. "Them's nothing. I 'loofah' them away. Look at my hairdo. People tell me I resemble Connie Stevens."

"Who?" I asked.

"The movie star. The actress that once married Eddie Fisher."

"Never heard of her," I said.

"Jeez, where you been hiding? Jeez, it's a hot night and lots of stars are out. Why don't we go over to your place and talk a little baseball, honey?"

When we were set to leave, Joyce just opened the front milk cooler and hollered in to Honeydew, "We're going!"

"Have fun, Joycey. Call me tomorrow," Honeydew yelled from behind the 2%.

I got a Stroh's twelve-pack for the ride. She followed me in her car. I cracked open a beer, turned up the radio, thought of what I'd do to Joyce. Things ain't so bad, I told myself.

She was giggling when she arrived. "I don't much watch sports," she said. "Say, I know where it was! I heard you on radio. You know that Biff Barton guy you see around at groshery stores?"

"He's my agent."

"He was on radio advertising Goody's, wa'n't he?"

"Sure, I been on radio with him. Why don't you whisper so we don't wake the neighbors."

"Thas where I heard you," she said.

After drinking two on the way over, I had ten beers left. Joyce carried a few with her. One can fell from her purse, broke open, fizzed. We were in the third-floor hallway of my apartment building. "I'm destined for the Polish-American Sports Hall of Fame, you know," I whispered, unlocking the door. "What you wearing under that blouse?"

"Oh hush," she said.

A Yoo-Hoo and three beers later and the blouse was on the floor. It was 1 A.M.; I figured Ellie was home, and Joyce, Honeydew's friend from the convenience store, was dancing to Merle Haggard's "Mama Tried" playing on my stereo. What was I doing? *Crazy with failure. Treadwell called me "Kielbasa" . . . "Sausage hands." I'd lost my hitting eye. I was trying to get it back with this Joyce lady.*

"What's the matter?" she asked when I didn't want to dance right off.

"Nothing. I want to drink. Ain't been feeling so hot lately and I just want another beer. Let's talk about something before we dance."

"Talk! What am I goin' to tell Honeydew? Oh yeah, Honeydew, he was a great guy. We just talked all night. Hon, I'm thirty years old. Well, twenty-nine. I've done enough talking. I want romance."

"Lemme just finish my beer."

"No, get up and dance with me. You must know them all. Wa-a-a Wa-Watusi."

"You know anything about ancient Egypt?" I said.

"Yeah, that you've got a mummy's curse put on you tonight. I've known guys like you all my life. Flashy big-with-the-talk-guys until you're alone. Then Boris Karloff. Look at me. Jeez, I've been told I'm beautiful."

When she lowered her head to my shoulder, I felt the stiff hair. It was peroxided blonde, I guess it's called. When she tried to smile seductively, the skin on her face pulled tight. It was like her face couldn't do what her heart wanted.

"Jeez, don't put your hands on my face like you're testing it or something. Jeez, what do you think—I had a facelift? Jeez, why don't you kiss me at least?"

Her lips didn't move much when she talked. When I kissed them, she couldn't make them move either. She said her name was Joyce Gott.

"Hush a minute," she said between beers. "I thought I heard something."

"You musta just heard a car. Maybe it's my agent's."

"Someone's at the door."

"There's nothing," I said. "Let's dance. There's nothing outside, Joyce. C'mon," I said real fast. "You know how to 'Limbo Rock'?"

"It's the '90s, hon. The limbo went out when I was a teenager. I mean I *heard* it was a '60s dance. I think they play it on Oldies stations sometimes."

"I don't care. Turn up the music. Here, I'll find a song. Go ahead. Limbo. I'll hum it. How l-o-o-o-w can you go-o-o?"

"No. Listen! You got an 'Augie' here in this building? Is that you?" Joyce said.

"Augie?" the plaintive voice outside the door said.

"The hell!" Joyce said. "You told me Race. Who's this Augie?"

"I'm telling you, my name's Race Gentry. Lemme call my agent to see. There's no one at the door. There's an Augie upstairs, come to think of it. He's a bartender."

When Joyce, half naked, opened the door, I tried to push it shut. The neighbors were standing in bathrobes, angry, murmuring to each other. They'd been awakened by Ellie beating on doors calling mournfully for "Augie."

"Don't disturb me," I said to her as I stepped outside. "Get out of here now like you're supposed to do when I'm busy, Ellie. What you doing here? I had a hard day. Tell all these folks to go back in their apartments."

"I'm pregnant," Queen Nefertiti was saying. She was crying.

"Well I had a damn hard day. I'm trying to relax."

"Race, are you really an all-star?" Joyce was saying, popping her head out from inside the apartment. "Who's this weeping beauty?"

"An all-star with one homer? He's had one round-tripper in two months," said Mr. Youngblood from downstairs.

I thought Ellie was gonna faint.

"*One?*" Joyce said. "One home run?"

The other neighbors started in. When he wasn't ogling Joyce, Jack Wright said I was an all-star fool. When I looked back in, Joyce was fixing her blouse, grabbing her purse. "You told me the name Race Gentry meant fifty home runs. Who's this out here callin' for you? Are you *married?*" Joyce hissed.

Poor Ellie, pregnant, looked deathly white when Joyce rushed past.

Drunker than I thought, I tripped on the stairs, could've permanently hurt myself, hurt my throwing arm. "No one was here, Ellie," I was yelling. "I was alone. You're seein' things."

Jeezus, I thought, when I didn't have my car keys. By the time I fished them out of my pocket, both gals were gone. Driving as fast as I could, head spinning, I went by Corky's Townhouse South Restaurant, past Morgan Coffee, Shreve City Gulf. As I looked for Ellie and Joyce, I wondered what a Polack from Yankeeland was doing mixed up with Connie Stevens and Ellie Pleasaunt in Louisiana. Why hadn't I been assigned to Triple-A International League Buffalo, a good Polish town, or Double-A Scranton-Wilkes-Barre?

Hung over, out of gas, I had on KEEL-Radio when the sun came up. I waited for Mr. Barton's voice over the radio to tell me what to do. If he'd said, "Go to Winn-Dixie, buy a hundred packages of Goody's," I would have. If he'd told me, "Go to Wal-Mart, greet people in my name," I would have done that. I had no one else now, and he knew how to call the Game of Life with fifty thousand watts behind him.

When I phoned, Ellie was at Hattie's.

"I'm out on King's Highway," I told Ellie when I got her to come to the phone. "It isn't what you think."

"I don't want to bother with you anymore," she said.

"What can I do all day without you?"

"I can't talk. Hattie's gotta get to work," she said, hanging up.

When I got Joyce on the phone, she hung up, too. She'd telephoned around town. Made a lot of calls about me. Maybe called Fair Grounds Field. "I fooled you anyway, Augie Gentry or whatever your name is," Joyce said. "Because I'm pushing fifty and you didn't notice." She called me "Sausage Glove" and slammed down the phone.

Then it was just me, Augie Wyzinski, listening to the dial tone. I waited and waited for Mr. Biff Barton's voice over the radio, over the phone. Jesus, I needed the sound of him for a minute to straighten me out. Nothing came on the radio, just ads for Pamida, Farmer Brown's Chicken, a few country songs, more ads. Where was talk radio? I went through a tank of gas between 7 A.M. and 1 P.M. driving Louisiana Avenue, I-20, then on the Barksdale Highway to Bossier. "Do you know Biff Barton?" I asked anyone I saw. "Where can I find Biff, the Voice of the Captains?"

Messed up in the head as I was now, I remembered Ellie talking about gardenias that bloomed in front of her folks' house. On January days you could smell them through the window, she'd said.

"Mama was hinting you should come back here in winter. Come see us," I remember Ellie saying. "If you don't, I'll send you a gardenia up north." She took my hand then. "You'll have a gardenia in the snow to remind you of me."

I recalled it so well. *What had happened in two months?* Thinking of Ellie and her parents as I sat in a parking lot in the rising August heat broke my heart. They were only seventy miles away. I turned the radio on, listening for Mr. Biff Barton. Where was he, a voice that in summer came out of the very heart of the country where you were . . . a voice that told you there's this field under a blue sky where an organ can be heard, where people cheer, yell, and grow lonely in the late innings of losing games or toward the end of the season when autumn is coming? This same voice tells you a catcher has responsibilities. He backs up first on infield ground balls, blocks wild pitches, explodes from the crouch to gun down the base stealers of this world. But I couldn't do it, couldn't get it done on the field, and now I'd blown it with the only girl who ever mattered to me.

By two o'clock it was a hundred degrees out. It looked like rain. On the dirt road that leads to Bayou Clarence I listened to heat bugs . . . watched the cattle egrets stepping gently in the water. I was sick. I do not know why a man does such things as I'd done. Why he cannot be faithful to one who loves him. Is it the price of fame? When you think you're above every citizen of Caddo Parish, Louisiana, because you're on a record home run streak, can you hurt and disregard them?

"Kielbasa. From now on you're Augie Kielbasa," the skipper'd said a month earlier. "Why don't you wear a sausage to catch with? Wear one on your head while you're at it."

From that night in Little Rock, Midland, or wherever it was through the whole last half of the Texas League season, I meant nothing to Mr. Treadwell with my .060 average and twenty passed balls.

A Christian man, the skipper would always say, "Morals is important and my boys gotta be good men—on the diamond and off. Always cherish the temple. Honor the temple. You live right and good off the field, you'll play right and good on the field. Thas all we ask, boys. Don't let no weakness of soul and heart destroy you in this game and in the Game of Life."

I guess he knew why *my* game had suffered. I'd struggled to get my hitting eye back, but it was like everything I'd done acting so crazy with women and drinking made me lose my edge. I'd forget what signal I just gave. A pitch in the dirt wouldn't get blocked. Thinking about it all made it worse. What about folks waiting for news of me in the *Evening Telegram* back home? How could I let them down?

By now it was 3:30. I was exhausted from the long day, not to mention the crazy night before. I missed Ellie so much. I turned the car around to head to the stadium for tonight's ball game against the

Arkansas Travelers. I was done in with regret and shame. I feared for the future. What would come of me?

Since mid-July, when I'd become the bullpen catcher, I heard the skipper Treadwell and Biff Barton talking as I warmed up the pitcher before games. Today when I got to the park, the Voice of the Captains seemed to know I'd been searching the dial for his voice—but he spoke to the skip as if nothing had happened.

"After the weekend only six games left," Biff was saying.

"We'll probably have El Paso in the playoffs, Biffy," the skipper was saying. Turning to me, he said, "Kid, you're startin'. Les us get a game out of you tonight." Some of his tobacco spit landed by me.

"Looks plum wore out," said Biff Barton. "Keepin' your nose clean, kid?"

Feeling pretty ragged, I didn't say nothing back.

"It's gonna rain," said the skipper. "I cain't risk the new young kid come in last week. The big club when they sent us Siveney last week told us 'Go easy . . . don't hurt Siveney. Get him in his playing time, but don't hurt him. He's a real prospect.' Les us just see what Augie's got or ain't got. Dry off from the drizzle, Kielbasa-hands. You're startin' tonight. You aren't too tired, are you?"

"I had some trouble with my girlfriend last night."

"Moral trouble?" the skip said. "Baptist trouble?"

"How'd you know?"

"Don't they teach you how to play it straight up north?" he asked. "Thas a problem."

As he stared at me, the rain started. I strapped on shin guards, chest protector, mask . . . the so-called "tools of ignorance" because only a fool crouches behind home plate. The Voice of the Captains yelled to me he was going to transmit my name to thousands of fans. He hung out his banner. KEEL-Radio would simulcast in Polish and English, he said, the first-ever Polish-English broadcast of a Texas League game.

Then I heard the crowd, organist, vendors, and heard Mr. Barton start his broadcast with observations on the catcher, 00. And I knew all the members in the National Polish-American Sports Hall of Fame in Orchard Lake, Michigan, were listening, waiting for me to join them. I'd read about them, seen programs Uncle Louie sent from the induction ceremonies: Stan "the Man" Musial in 1973; Ted Kluszewski in '74; in '75, Aloysius Harry Szymanski (Simmons), who was voted MVP with the Philadelphia A's and the next year, 1930, won the batting crown; Stan (Kowalewski) Coveleski in '76 . . . on and on, Eddie (Lopatynski) Lopat, Bill Mazeroski, Bill "Moose" Skowron, Tony Kubek . . .

5.
HOPEFUL FUTURE HALL OF FAMER
SEES PLANS CHANGE

At 8:34 I struck out. It was the sixth inning. KEEL's every watt carried it. When Treadwell came out, the public address system switched to polkas. There was "Pennsylvania Polka," "She's Too Fat Polka," "Liechtensteiner Polka." Fans groaned and started chanting "Ban Polka! Ban Polka!"

"I cain't put in no one else before the playoffs because orders from the big club tell me to keep Siveney benched on rainy nights so he don't hurt his arm or twist his knee," the skipper said through the rain. "So what do I do? You're good for nothin', Kielbasa. Even your music stinks."

As the grounds crew unrolled the tarp in the rain that was falling harder now, Treadwell's face got redder and redder. Someone had told him what happened with Joyce. He didn't like embarrassment by his players. Rain dripping from his cap, he cussed, spit his tobacco. Was Biff analyzing my life-moves?

How do you go back to local programming, you wonder in the

rain with the last polka playing? Some other night in years to come the skipper will be chewing tobacco, Biff Barton saying, "Good evening, Caps fans," the stadium vendors hawking their goods while cars and trucks on Highway I-20 outside the ballpark whip across America as usual. It's like nothing ever changes down there. *What will Ellie be doing that night, talking to someone else about flowers? As she reads the paper, will her eye catch a story on the Shreveport Captains? Will her ma ask, "Ellie, do you ever think of that nice young man from up north? Your father asks about him from time to time." Will Ellie tell her, "No, Mama, not much anymore . . . But look how nice the gardenias are blooming."* Now there was an empty stadium. The rain they'd predicted all day was forming puddles and streams behind home plate when I saw Ellie walking through the box seats of section C, blouse and pink summer sweater soaked.

"Why didn't I keep you a secret?" she was asking, wiping rain from her forehead. I knew she was no ghost. She was down on the field now. Only two other people were left in the ballpark.

"I shouldn't have taken you to meet my parents this summer." She was running her hands along the screen behind home; and I was thinking how, when I'd first gone to Natchitoches with Ellie, her mother and father had said, "Sit down, young man, we saved you a place." It'd all changed by late August. Ellie was saying, "I want to get away from here. I'll apologize at home to my folks, apologize to Hattie—"

The groundskeeper was talking to Mr. Barton. They surprised us. Standing in the shadows, they looked like a part of the ballpark.

"Leave the lights on for them?" the groundskeeper was asking.

"Sure," the Voice of the Captains said.

From under the umbrella the groundskeeper held for him, Biff Barton yelled over, "Kid, you know this might be it for you? If you were famous here and hitting .330, they'd forgive you for fooling around with all those women. But with the way you've gone . . . Next year fans are going to ask, 'Where's the Polish boy? We don't see 00. Where's Kielbasa Kid?' 'He got released,' I'll have to say."

"I know. Tell 'em I'll tend bar up north or sweep floors at the flour mill like my dad does. I can practice my swing in the boiler room for a comeback. I'll get a tryout somewhere."

"You come live down here and straighten out," Mr. Barton was saying. "Stay here, kid. Start a life where you'll pause at the screen door after work . . . dream of what might've been if you'd gotten the extra base hit in Tulsa. Then you can go inside, see her fixing your supper and how beautiful she is no matter what she's doing, and be glad you have turned into a hardworking Christian who once had a shot at the big show. There's one decent thing to do, Wyzinski. Why not stay south here, work for the cotton oil plant or for that little college in Natchitoches? Cut grass for the college till you get settled. Maybe when the Caps release you, you can take responsibility—fix car radiators for Ates Radiator or something. We've all made mistakes."

"I wonder if I can, Mr. Barton. Maybe I could get into the insurance business," I said, thinking to myself that "moral prospects" is what the skip and Mr. Barton were wanting us to be—good players with clear consciences who didn't have defects of soul and heart, defects that would hurt them no matter what they did in life.

When I saw beautiful Ellie still standing in the rain, I believed there was hope if she'd give me a chance to change my life. She was smoothing the wet hair from her face, listening to Biff.

"Then you got a kid steps in like this one they protected, this straight-arrow, nondrinking, nonwomanizing prospect Siveney," Biff Barton was saying. "Kid, most folks aren't going anyplace in life but the feed store, the insurance business, the lumber mill day in and day out. They're just ordinary moral folks. It's raining tonight, so they're home. They've got families. Tomorrow they'll go to work, struggle along, pay the bills. Are you going to join us?"

"Sure," I said.

When Mr. Barton held his fingers like an umpire signaling the count, I was thinking how I'd once hit safely in eight straight games. *That* should mean something to God and the Blessed Virgin.

"Three and two. Runner at first is going," Mr. Barton said. "This pitch could decide it." When he said that, he turned on his heel and walked away.

The rain came so hard then I thought Ellie and I'd be washed off the field. She was looking at the frightening sky. "You shouldn't have come to Natchitoches. You got my folks believing in us," she said.

"Tell them I didn't want it to turn out wrong."

"It don't matter now," she said.

When she told me she never loved me—not even at the start—her voice breaking, too, I knew I'd had my chance, that she'd given me her heart and I'd broken it and that she would go away. I'd turn into an immoral gaboosh who'd work in places like the Heartbreak, recalling the might-have-beens Biff Barton told me about.

"Too much is wrong with you," she was saying, crying. I didn't hear what else she said as she opened the gate by the dugout where the sign on the fence says: No Pepper Games.

When the Voice of the Captains and the groundskeeper escorted her through the dark runway beneath the stands, nobody asking whether I could do better, nobody giving me a second chance, I realized what remained was for them to shut off the lights on my chances for happiness with Ellie and on my one chance at making the Polish-American Sports Hall of Fame.

I sat all night in the dark stadium, regretting what would become of me. Lots of people hurt and betray others. She didn't deserve it. I should've valued her the way I valued making the Hall of Fame. I didn't think or know much last season. But it hits me now that these memories are the tools of ignorance I am left with, so I put them on and I regret who I am.

6.

EX–MINOR LEAGUER JOINS
COUNTY BEER LEAGUE

A season later, I wipe the bar at the Heartbreak and turn the radio dial when the jukebox is off. Over the airwaves of the South last year, signals were crisscrossing, bringing me together with folks like Mr. and Mrs. Pleasaunt, like Ellie, like Biff . . . good, ordinary folks. Folks who lived plain, quiet lives. A life in Louisiana would've been perfect for me, too: Captains broadcasts, the summer skies Biff Barton talked about, Ellie on walks by Cane River, reminding me of my hitting streaks and pulling out newspaper clippings she'd once saved about me. There'd be faithful church attendance and a baby to love and rear. *Oh, Ellie, I've learned what I never knew last season: you were trusting and honest and I let you down. I looked for a flower this January, but you didn't send one.*

Nowadays till someone at the end of the bar—till Pete, say—needs the services of a washed-up ballplayer (of a gaboosh like him), I imagine a voice a long ways off in the rain. I can hear you, Ellie, walking away with that voice from the radio I knew so well.

Nowadays, circling the bases in the Old Timers' League up here in Douglas County, wearing this wool uniform in Sunday's heat, I think of you. For each rocket I hit, the owner of Heartbreak buys me a Fitger's beer and a package of string cheese. My signing bonus was a job here and Sundays off to hit homers for you and me, the catcher and you, Ellie—who will never be together after last year's season of lies. I hit home runs of a kind never seen before. You can believe this. Home runs that tear out my heart, home runs that are talked about in this league of nobodies.

"Augie?"

"Yeah, Pete?" I say.

"What ya thinkin' about?"

"Nothing," I say. "A girl."

"Who?"

"I'll tell you later, but now I'm gonna think about runners I threw out in Jackson, of the great two-hit game I called for Tim Crow in Midland-Odessa. A catcher has responsibilities, you know, Pete."

I shake his hand as he slumps against the wall. I shake all their hands. My East End fans. The Hamm's clock ticks on, the sign sizzles. The gabooshes shuffle to the jukebox, the men's room, the pachinko game to try to roll a nickel down the right path. Things never change at Heartbreak Hotel.

"Thanks," I say to them, to ham-faced Wladziu, to Stashu, to Benny.

"Dziękuję," they say. "You had a goot career in basebull."

"Thank you, Paul," I say.

"Yeah, Augie."

"Thank you, too, Casimir."

"You bet, Augie. Glad you're home."

"Thank you, John."

"Tank *you,* Augie. Strike three for you?"

"Here's a toast to all you guys for telling me how bad I was at the game," I say. "Next we're getting the neon sign fixed. I'll talk to the boss. We aren't heartbroke, so why should we have a broken sign? Well, maybe Pete is. Pete, you're pickled. Why don't you go home? Can you walk or should I call you a cab?"

"*You* go home!"

"I can't. What would I do? Sit with my ma? Say the rosary with her? Anyway, if I looked in the mirror at home, I'd just see you guys. I might as well stay here where I got you in front of me. Go on, tell me I'm lousy. I got all night to listen to you guys with high self-esteem."

Bird of Passage

After the funeral, the loneliness started. What now? thought Papa Wladek on wind-bitten afternoons when he'd wash his frying pan and put away the bread and horseradish. December cold settled in the morning of his wife's funeral; snow covered the bouquets at her gravesite. Now old age stretched before him. As he left for lunch in the church basement, he saw in the hall mirror a widower in charcoal gray slacks, brown cardigan, and beige car coat with rabbit's fur collar: a lonely man, Wladek Czypanski, now that his wife was gone.

"Stay for UNO. Play a hand of Spite and Malice," the "golden-agers" said after lunch in the church hall, which he attended for their company, but by then he wanted to leave. At home, however, things just irritated him. Neighbors brought goulashes, booyas, and salmon loaves to the back door. "The bulki rolls . . . all you do is heat them," they'd say. He'd spoon their delicacies into the garbage. Outside in the snow he noticed footprints passing from Leo Polaski's yard to his, Wladek's, then to the other neighbor's yard. Wladek had asked the newspaper carrier not to walk through the yard of a nonsubscriber— another irritant. Then the phone rang with salesmen wanting to sell a headstone for Martha's grave. As Wladek hung up, reaching absent-

mindedly into the cupboard for coffee or into a drawer for a spoon, he
was startled by the cold of these places. In downstairs closets whose
doors he kept shut, in cupboards and drawers, it seemed much colder
than in the center of his house. He'd gone without facing the cold for
fifty years: Martha, the kids, work, his other obligations keeping him
busy. Now the house had grown so cold there was nothing to do but
sit by the space heater waiting for Martha.

You see these widowed men all over—at bus stops or paying their
market and utility bills or sitting in the corners of the public library
sorting papers. Perhaps they've come to copy their wives' death certifi-
cates on the photocopy machine or to look in phone books for the
names of old friends. These widowers appear so vulnerable when
they finally realize they are alone that you think a sudden wind will
blow them away; yet after crying all night, the next day they often
come to Mass or to lunch in the church basement fully in possession
of themselves. By early January, Wladek Czypanski could make it back
from Communion without crying, could shuffle through the lunch
line now without sobbing over the kapusta or the dinner rolls.

When his Martha was alive and now when he had time to think, he
wondered—quite against his will, you understand—whether he could
be passionate with women. To avoid temptation when she was alive,
he'd help his wife in little ways about the house or go to confession. Yet
the thought of passion returned when he read the *"Pozna"* section of a
newspaper he received in the mail, where lonely middle-aged men
advertised:

> *Kawaler, finansowo niezależny, wysoki, lubiący dom i prodróże . . .*
> Tall, financially secure bachelor who likes to travel or stay at home
> seeks acquaintanceship . . . Write P.O. Box———.

For a faithful man like Wladek, what was there to do but hold
himself in check? Had he telephoned one of the numbers listed under

"Marriage Services/Companionship," his wife might have asked, "Who are you talking to on the telephone, Wladek?" What could he reply, "To the *Polsko-Amerykańskie Biuro Matrymonialne* in Chicago arranging Friendship, Love, Possibly Marriage"? Still, thoughts of women came to mind. Don't most husbands think about treating someone new to a breakfast or to pork hocks at the East End Cafe? Wladek Czypanski's dreams had been splintered like frost on the window of his lost youth; and now, with her gone, how guilty he felt for having strayed in his mind.

In April he placed an ad in the *"Pozna"* section of the *dziennik chicagowski*:

Zamożny, 68-letni Amerykanin pozna szczupłą panią, zdecydowaną na dzielenie wspólnego życia. Well-off gentleman, youthful side of 68, wishing to make acquaintance of slender single or widowed woman to share my life and house. Tel. 715-555-3606.

He received a phone call from a woman in Waukegan who coughed a lot.

He tried another advertisement in the *dziennik*:

Samotny?
Deserted? Alone?
Call *Pan* Wladek
Tel: 715-555-3606

Nothing.

He tried a "Bureau," The Venus Club, which advertised itself as "Professional and Discreet," offering services such as *"Przyjaźń* (cozy conversation and fantasy talk)," *"Miłość* (love)," *"Małzenstwo* (marriage)."* In their ad, a pretty woman was holding a telephone receiver. Wladek imagined her hot, red lips whispering to him, "Finally Something New, Something Special. Polish-Speaking Girls. *Erotyczny, Seks, Romantyczny."*

"Hallo? Hallo?" Mr. Czypanski said. "I have to speak quickly." The passion he got cost him a $230.00 phone bill, but he was left unsatisfied. What good was this fantasy telephone? he wondered.

"Papa, we can't get through to you anymore," his daughters said when they'd finally managed to telephone him from Syracuse.

"It's this funeral business. Bills to straighten out tie up the phone. I'm okay."

Hanging up, he went to sleep hoping to forget how things had changed. He remembered when signs in the neighborhood read *Walczyka Rzeźnictwo, Czerwone Jabłuszko, Dom Ziednoczenia*. There were markets, lodges, clubrooms; dancing in the parish hall. People got together in those days. In the taverns you'd see dock workers and millhands, ore, coal, or flour dust on their clothes. All the men had sisters or daughters—and Wladek Czypanski, a virile, dust-free man, was the Prince of East Fifth Street. But what now?

No one sponsored church dances anymore. Most of the markets and bakeries where you'd meet people were gone out of business. Now when he'd catch the lingering scent of Martha's perfume as he rummaged through the cabinets or closets of her room, he'd hold the sleeve of her sweater or housecoat and think of her and feel guilty for dreams he'd had of women and sin.

When the worst loss and pain, the worst of winter, passed, he improved. He could eat again, play UNO at church. Forgetting the phone calls he'd made to the *"Erotyczny"* fantasy line and the urges he'd felt to place advertisements, he stepped into the sunlit yard to talk to neighbors. Apple trees blossomed.

"You'll have good fruit," he told Leo Polaski.

"Lot to clean up, though," said the neighbor. "It's a mess when they fall."

To the other neighbor, Wesolewski, Wladek said, "How's the boy doing in college?"

"Fine. Haven't seen you much, Wladek."

"Spring weather again. I'll be out more."

What renewed Wladek as much as the longer, sunnier days occurred one morning when Mrs. Kosmatka said in Polish after Mass at St. Adalbert's, "Wladek, get your head up. *Pani* Czypanska has been gone long enough. You write my niece."

He'd been thinking of doing just that when, to his surprise, a letter arrived a week later from Poland. "Tell me of the wonderful strawberries in your garden," it read.

He touched a drop of strawberry juice to the corner of an envelope and began a reply. "Dear *Pani* Slavik," he wrote to her:

I'm widowed. I'll introduce myself: *Pan* Wladek. How do you do? I lost my wife seven months ago. Your aunt said, "Write my niece in Old Country." So here I am—Wladek. I'll tell you, Ewa, if I may call you by your first name in Polish, the weather here is pretty bad. Autumn is usually nice, though. Last autumn before she died (only God knows the suffering!) my Martha and I went to a waterfall near town, the highest one in our state of Wisconsin. A light breeze started a million pieces of gold to flutter and fly across the vast, deep gorge when my beloved and sadly missed wife and I were looking into the falls. They were aspen leaves we saw glitter in sunlight.

Wladek Czypanski

Very soon a letter arrived from Poland. Wladek found Mrs. Kosmatka. On her knees weeding her garden, she said, "You write to her again. Wait. I haf picture in apron pocket."

"Dear *Pani* Slavik," Wladek wrote:

How beautiful your hair. It's not easy to tell the color of your eyes, though, in the photo—blue, hazel? Your aunt says you're 29. I wonder if you have marriage in mind? Many are after *Pan* Wladek in America, but alas I have no interest. I'm surprised someone so lovely as yourself has "escaped" marriage in your country. I wonder whether the mock orange blossom I send maintains its scent when you receive humble Wladek's love. . . .

The letter came out twice as long as the first. That evening he stored his wife's clothes in boxes in the garage.

"My Beloved," began Ewa's return letter, "I am so lonely in Poland. . . ."

Now when he worked in the yard, he kept a window open in case the phone rang. Three women answered the *dziennik* ad. When none of them wished to move two area codes away from Chicago, Wladek spent a week on a letter to Mrs. Kosmatka's niece, then went to the priest. "Is there sin in this when my wife died so recently?" Wladek asked.

When another, in fact two more letters arrived from Poland, Wladek consulted a travel agent.

How he bustled about now. Though a little late in the growing season, he planted tomatoes and squash. He had his hair cut twice, bought a new suit and pair of shoes, traded his snap-brim cap for a hat with a feather. Mrs. Kosmatka gave him a rutabaga cut up in finger-length pieces to eat for the trip. Ewa'd written saying she'd received the money.

On downstate the widower traveled, carrying a cardboard sign he'd made with his name in colored ink. Entering Illinois on the airport charter bus he'd boarded in Madison, Wladek noticed the country grow strange. He was no fool. He kept repeating, "Don't stare at colored people. Don't gawk, Wladek, no matter how big the O'Hare Airport." He wore a suit, the feathered hat. He was, he thought, better dressed than most in the terminal, where people chattered, airport carts slid weary travelers through crowds, planes took off outside.

To practice, he held the cardboard sign over his head: WLADEK CZYPANSKI. If your daughters saw you, Wladek, he thought as jet engines screeched. Crossing himself, he lifted the cardboard sign, pushed toward the gate with the others. WE'RE NOT THE ONLY WAY TO GET HERE FROM WARSAW, BUT WE'RE THE FASTEST. *LOT POLISH AIRLINES*, another sign read. He straightened his tie, took a quarter from his pocket for the telephone. On the other end, he heard an accordion in the background, then a woman's voice saying, *"Erotyczny, Seks, Romantyczny."*

"It's Wladek. The one you say is so sexy. You know, middle-aged Wladek. Charge my account. My sweetheart is coming off the plane from Warsaw nonstop. Do I wait a week or longer for *erotyczny?*" As passengers crowded customs—old and young, students, priests, businesswomen—he wrote down his instructions; how he was to bow as he kissed her hand, what he was to whisper later, what perfume he was to buy her. The woman on the other end said Wladek was "hot" and "sexy."

When only a few people remained, he raised the sign again.

She was standing in a corner, looking about, travel bag over her shoulder. Her hair lay braided atop her head. She had green eyes, pale lips the dark lipstick failed to conceal. Seeing her healthy complexion, he pulled his hat over his wrinkled forehead.

"How do you do?" he said, raising the sign that read WLADEK.

"Did you brink your car, Mr. Wladek?" she asked.

"I was afraid to drive to Chicago. It's twelve-hour drive. We have to take a 'local' bus back. It stops in every town so you can see Wisconsin."

"Put down the sign. I'm here. Why you do that?" she said.

Her voice made him dumb with happiness.

On the trip back she yawned, stared through the windows, slept. He wanted to touch her hair, but wouldn't for fear of waking her. When she awoke enough for him to ask for a kiss, she lifted the hat from his lap and kissed the feather. What long days the two of them had had, he thought, never so relieved to see the sign LEECHES . . . SUCKERS welcoming the bus into Superior off Highway 53. After bait

shops came a mile of gas stations, motels, and wild rice stands, then the
ore docks, the coal yard, the packing plant, the Fredericka Flour Mill.

Wladek's house was fine, Ewa thought; Superior, Wisconsin, and
the East End fine. Once they'd rested—Wladek sleeping in his recliner-
rocker, Ewa occupying the bedroom—they celebrated their union, old
man and youthful beauty, with a candlelight ceremony at St. Adalbert's
followed by a small dinner in the back dining room of the Holiday Inn.

"Love is the Lord's institution whereby He provides for the propagation of mankind," the priest said, raising a toast.

The groom raised his glass. Downing the champagne and thinking
of his new bride preparing for propagation, Wladek ordered potato
pancakes. Between forkfuls, he patted her hands and whispered in
Polish what they'd told him to over the phone. No recliner-rocker for
him tonight, he thought.

When one of the guests sang, Wladek and his wife danced, Wladek
feeling the soft temptation of her breasts, the luscious curve of her hips
and waist, the sensuous touch of her knee against his. "O how we
danced on the night we were wed," the singer went on. Other East End
old-timers danced with Ewa until at last everyone sang the Polish toast
"*Sto lat!* May you live a hundred years!" to the sweethearts in their bliss.

With the priest's and guests' farewells still warming his heart, he
unlocked the front door of his house. When his wife slipped away, he
wetted and combed his hair in the bathroom, checked to see that his
shave was holding up, and, as final preparation for the consummation
of marriage, brushed and cleaned his dentures, hiding the Efferdent
and the Poli-Grip when he was through.

"Sweet Bird," he called down the hallway. Satisfied he was up to the
task, he called again, "Ewa, Sweet."

He found her sleeping beneath the percale sheets. He nudged her,
whispered.

"Go 'way," she muttered.

"Let us be one," he said.

"Oh Stanislaw, oh Januszka, oh Antek," she whispered men's names.

"No, it's Wladek."

"Wladek?"

When she responded, he smiled, knowing he'd not lost so much of his youthful appeal for her. Though his knee and shoulder cracked when he crawled beside her and though he feared, when he assumed the "male-dominant position," that his upper plate might fall out on her despite the Poli-Grip, he hoped she would be too tired after her trip to notice. And how right he was. The Wladek of old—fearless woman-tamer—now lurched twice, called "Kitten! Kitten!" in a high, squeaky voice, and fell asleep in an instant, Ewa herself never quite having awakened to his charms except once when, thinking she was still aboard the flight from Warsaw, she dreamt an engine burst into flame, a wing broke, and—at the moment the plane crashed into the sea—these red and white things like false teeth dropped from somewhere high above her—heaven perhaps.

In the weeks after the night of passion and bliss, Ewa began staying up later, rising around eleven o'clock in the morning after he'd been in the kitchen drinking coffee or outside tending the tomato and squash garden. When through the open window he heard her rousing, yawning, and stretching for ten minutes, he scrambled inside for his teeth.

"You let your nails grow. All day you shine them," he joked after a month.

"Something in here's making me sick . . . your house? Or is it you?" she sighed.

Summer afternoons now he'd ask Ewa Slavik as she rested in the big, cool bed, "Dearest, may I turn on the lamp with the blue silk shade?" If she said yes, he'd next implore her to throw back the percale sheets.

Things weren't going so well, though. Brushing her hair, she'd sometimes toss a summer shawl, a blouse, anything around her bare shoulders.

"*Idyota!* Don't look at me," she'd say. Then he'd catch her touching her lips to the mirror to see whether they had the right bow.

Other times when he'd pick a goblet of raspberries from his bushes, she'd leave them untasted on the dresser. This is not how *"Erotyczny"* told me it would be, he thought. *"Erotyczny"* told me I was the best lover who'd ever paid to talk to them.

How beautifully her fingers and hands wore Wladek's rings and bracelets; how like apple blossoms the smell of the light hair Ewa Slavik pulled from her neck so he could fit expensive gold chains around it. In the Warsaw Tavern and the Kosciuszko Lodge, they laughed at him. "Our fathers emigrated *za chleb,* 'for bread,'" they'd say. "This woman of Wladek's comes for the streets of gold." No one spared Wladek. Everyone in the neighborhood (perhaps even Mrs. Kosmatka) knew what Wladek didn't: that Ewa was a bird of passage. From the Old Country, such women write endearing words. Once yours in marriage they can stay in the United States—a house with a Mix-Master, a radio, a neck pillow, a hair dryer, a space heater when the room gets cold; these things in exchange for a year or two with a doddering, retired East End millhand who soaks his teeth.

"Why do you so much look at the ground?" neighborhood women soon began to inquire of Wladek.

"Ewa says I'm tight with the money. I hang around her too much and make her cook. My house smells like kapusta, she complains."

"Niece is beautiful woman," said the aunt in Ewa's defense, "she feels odd in thees neighborhood. No young people here to go dancing."

The sad, beautiful Ewa Slavik *did* look bored and tired. Wladek, do this . . . Wladek, do that, she'd say. He wasn't allowed to answer "*nie*" to her. The day he tried she tore the feather from his hat.

* * *

On the anniversary of his beloved wife Martha's death, the cold returned. He realized then he was truly alone—worse yet, he now loved the second woman more than the first. When he tried reading a love poem by Juliusz Słowacki, one of Poland's great Romantic poets and who himself was tortured by the hopeless love of women, Ewa turned away, covered herself with blankets, anything to avoid Wladek. Slumped in his recliner, he wondered why trouble visited a decent man.

During winter, the house stayed cold. By Ash Wednesday, he asked, "Do we have the blue silk lampshade of love anymore, dear Ewa?"

"I wout like you to get money for me to spend," she said, neither mentioning the lampshade of love nor seeming to understand the American retiree's concept of a "fixed income."

"Besides my social security and pension, I have only—," then he stopped, thinking it better not to say.

When he gave her a few dollars, she'd turn on him the full light of her smile. How lucky the man who lost himself in her hair, he'd think, assuring himself the differences they had were minor in relation to their joy. He'd ask to feel her thighs, her hips. She'd look at his knobby fingers, always cold and stiff. "Come, then let me get you a new dress," he'd say.

During Easter Week, she said, "Wouldn't you get that necklace with the little diamonds for me? You can hide it in Easter basket. I'm alone in U.S. It would help."

Then it was something else, a brooch . . . a tiara.

Toward the beginning of May when a regime of warmer temperatures set up over the area, Wladek Czypanski appeared at his neighbor Charlie's door quite distraught. Wesolewski's son answered.

"Come into the kitchen, *Pan* Czypanski. I'll get my father," the boy said.

"I can't think," Wladek was saying, voice trailing off when Charlie Wesolewski came downstairs. "I'm a fool," he said. He spoke in Polish

about how he thought nothing worse could have visited him after
Martha's death.

"Is she sick?" asked Wesolewski. "Is she dying?"

"No, she left."

"When?"

"Two days ago after I read Słowacki to her."

Wladek, who'd removed the snap-brim cap he'd taken to wearing
again, now pulled it over his forehead. "I thought she was in her
room."

"You didn't look in for two days?" asked Wesolewski.

"I bought her a summer dress," Wladek said as if he hadn't heard.

He went to see Mr. Polaski. "You're sure she left, Wladek?" he
asked. Not wanting to cry in front of anyone, Wladek thought he'd
better go home from Leo Polaski's.

Gathering the strawberries that were growing in the yard, he
arranged them along her nightstand, turned the blue silk light on,
sprinkling Ewa's cologne on the bulb. "I'll go away to my nephew's in
Detroit," he told everyone in the neighborhood.

June passed. In early July, a postcard arrived of "The Sears Tower—
Chicago Skyline At Night." Who do I know in Chicago? he wondered.
As he had each summer day, he turned on the bedroom light, lay in her
bed, stared at the scapular and rosary hanging from her vanity. With
the evening birds singing, the man whose wife left him told the neighbors, "I've heard from her. She's thinking of me and knows the address
to come home to."

Now the neighborhood stopped paying attention. He'd told his
story so often even children knew how foolish he was. When the
mountain ash berries reddened, when the aspen leaves swirled above
the gorge, Wladek wrote to his wife at her address in Wrocław, Poland:
"I know you've thought of me faithfully, Ewa. I know your letters are
coming. They've been delayed somewhere. Do you remember our
foolish blue lamp? I drip berry juice on this letter to hide the tears shed
for you. Would you like to hear more from me?"

Though he'd been without beloved Martha for two years, how much longer the time without Ewa seemed. He created the delusion of hope that she was thinking of him. He'd never told Wesolewski or anyone that she had a checkbook to draw against his fixed income with. Was this not proof Ewa was his—that she relied on him like this? One day a canceled check arrived from a Chicago department store. "Wardrobe expenses," she'd written on the back.

Such hope saw him through winter. Reminders of the signs of a very positive change in things came each week in January and February: the winter wasn't as severe as others . . . a new paperboy was respecting his wishes, walking cheerfully on the sidewalk. Each month, too, Wladek wrote such letters as these to the Old Country:

I know yours are on their way, Dear One. I wrote you letters seven months ago, three months ago, and more often since. I don't know where else to send mine but to your mother. Your letters are being held. How long before they are sent? I hope you're enjoying your travel. Do you remember Wladek, his feather? In the night, Kitten, leaving my lonely recliner-rocker, I came to you. "Jan," you muttered, or "Stanislaw" as you opened your arms to me. You continued the deception, the hard-to-get deception, when in the "bridal bower" (to borrow from Słowacki) you saw who was stroking your strawberry: "Get out! Go away! You're not Jan! You're not Stanislaw! I'll pull your feather . . . burn it good. Put in your teeth!" you'd say. But I knew you were playing. I *can't* be wrong. I know you still love me.

Never before, in fact, had their love for each other seemed so real as on that first sunny day in March—March 4 to be exact, her birthday. He was out working on a patch of grass that was greening beside the house when he felt surely that right then she was thinking of him. There'd been a withdrawal from the bank, the largest yet, enough for a better necklace than he'd gotten her and for plane fare home to her beloved Papa Wladek. "I know you're preparing to return in style to show the peasants," he wrote. He even called *"Erotyczny"* to share his joy.

"Do you wish to speak to Jadwiga, Basia, or one of the other Polish-speaking girls?" the voice on the "fantasy line" asked. "We have newer, sexier girls now, too."

"No, no. My wife is coming home. It's Wladek Czypanski again. Let me tell you about my happiness in life."

"Stay on the line. Go on. Keep talking. Tell us your fantasies. Do you have clothes on? I'm wearing high heels. Do you like that, *Pan* Wladek? Do you need spanking?"

After an hour and a half of phone talk, he'd never been happier.

On another, yet warmer day when he was certain of seeing Ewa very, very soon, his neighbor called across the fence, "Look, Wladek!"

"What do you have?" he asked. "What is it, a pale thought for me?"

He saw a tiny bird beside an old fencepost. The bird was unfledged. No feathers.

"Where did it come from?" Wladek asked the neighbor Charlie.

"I don't know. We can't do anything about it."

What mysteries the Lord God holds, Wladek thought as he stored his hedge clippers in the garage atop a box of his first wife's clothes. Chores complete, he felt hopeful the mail would bring something. "Please, God, a message from Ewa," he prayed, pretending as he did that he was eyeing her sitting in the lawn chair he'd put out for her each day, Ewa naked except for harem pants, Ewa yawning, Ewa beckoning him.

He heard Charlie again. "There's something in your mailbox. Mailman must have come, Wladek."

"It's a letter. I know it is. She's sending money. Too risky carrying so much with her when she's getting ready to return to me for propagation." As he checked the mail, the fervor of his prayers increased.

When he was certain neither Charlie the neighbor nor anyone else could see him from their yards or kitchen windows, Wladek returned to his own backyard so, undisturbed, he could enjoy the moment alone with his sweet Ewa Slavik.

After all this waiting, his beloved bird of passage had finally longed for him enough to send another postcard. This one was from Chicago, too. This one had a business name stamped in the corner: *FANTASZJA NA TELEFON EROTYCZNY, SEKS, ROMANTYCZNY.* This one said she had a good job and included her business number. "Wladek," she'd scribbled. "Please call. Do it for your Ewa who sits here in love with many lonely men, though none of them like you. You're the best. Call me at this number. I'll give you a discount and make you so happy."

The World at War

1.

When I discover his seaman's card in a dresser drawer, I see there was hope in Antek's eyes. The mouth too—slightly open as the shutter clicked at the Coast Guard station in 1938—suggests movement, hopefulness, goodwill. I wonder whether my father had been encouraged by the photographer to smile and to say something in Polish, "*Ku morzu* . . . Seawards!" perhaps. Unwilling to risk so much of himself, he's compromised by parting his lips a little and laughing at the rumors of war.

This seaman's card tells a story I must learn to read. No doubt the crease occurred as the picture was glued to the card, for the face in the photo of long ago is split down the center. Below the forehead, the two-sided face doesn't match up. To the right of the left eyebrow and eye, the crease in the photo sinks, leaving the bridge of the nose untouched, then turning back over the left nostril, cutting through the middle of the mouth and chin before ending where the message below the chin reads: GENUINE ONLY IF WATERMARKED USCG. Through the entire war, my father carried the two-sided face in his billfold.

2.

Say it is now 1947. For five years Antek Dabrowski of Superior has made many serious sea voyages where he's witnessed the struck masthead of a ship breaking the water outside New York harbor, witnessed the SS *Alcoa Prospect* torpedoed and the SS *Julia Luckenbach* colliding with a British tanker, seen men burning in gasoline, men drifting helplessly toward the gasoline, observed a galley man violently afflicted with fear, a "nervous disorder," and put ashore in Liverpool, watched flares go off, felt his ship lose power and drop from a convoy.

Home again, Antek tries reflecting on his experience, but he's entered a different war now. Where is the time to think when he labors ten-hour days at the flour mill, then has his family responsibilities and a home to keep up? Skimming Samuel Eliot Morison's *History of United States Naval Operations in World War II*, he finds minor references to his merchant sea adventures in volume one, very little more in volume two. Five years transporting general cargo such as oleo, canned meats, flour, steel billets, trucks, and tires; coal for Genoa, ammunition for Mozambique—five dangerous years of it and, in 1,404 pages, Antek Dabrowski's and other merchant mariners' careers merit an 89-word paragraph in Morison's book.

Hoping to coax himself into the present of postwar America, he tries self-help, ordering study kits from *The Popular Educator* magazine and from International Correspondence Schools. (I was young. I remember father studying self-help.) Say it's 1949. If he improves his public speaking skills, if he keeps up on "The Theory of Alternating Currents" and "Industrial Motor Applications," and if he gets my mother's permission, then he will return to sea "self-improved," and there be happier now, more popular, perhaps advancing himself in the merchant service. He quits both courses after a few months, though. No time. Flour mill responsibilities. Too much real work for the reasonable man to complete his homework.

3.

1953: Now a few years later we go to my uncle's for *Victory at Sea*. My uncle Wladziu has the first television set on our block. Each week Antek looks for himself in black and white. When the music begins, the big white Victory "V" appears over gray, rolling seas, and Leonard Graves intones, "And now: 'Sea and Sand.' Hitler is on the brink of what Napoleon failed to do, conquer Russia . . ." When the narrator switches from the Murmansk run to another part of the sea war, Antek Dabrowski leans forward intently, watching for himself as a convoy of ships winds its way across the sea. "If the convoy doesn't make it," Graves says, "all of North Africa will fall."

"Quiet. Hush," says Antek. "*There* was a war! I tell you I saw a freighter covered with monkeys. I saw a cook go berserk. Too much hashish and arrack in Guantanamo Bay. I saw U-boats chase my convoy just past the submarine nets in New York."

Stuck in the flour mill though yearning for the sea, my father inquires about marine employment. In letters he explains to prospective employers that, formerly an engine-room operator at Fredericka Flour, he's been given a lower pay classification when operators' jobs are lost to automation, even then a sign of the American future. He wants to be a fireman or oiler on the lakes again. "I'm 39 years old, in good health, a married parent and homeowner," he writes, explaining how, before demotion to packer-loader, he'd "maintained the mill's steam boilers, pumps, and air compressors." He mentions old firing and oiling days for the M. A. Hanna Steamship Company and his war service in the Atlantic and Mediterranean. The Great Lakes shipping companies, every one, respond that their policy is to "hire *new* wipers and oilers, then have them progress through the fleet." So there is no hope for my father.

Had Antek looked in those days, he'd have seen grain dust coloring his hair and filling the wrinkles around his eyes. In a mirror in a quiet room, he might have said, "You're Antek. You've been to sea. You work in a flour mill. Antek, Antek, what are you hoping for?" A lesser man— or a braver one—might have observed the gray, disappointed face. He might have admitted his day had come and gone, and that now it was his son's turn to make history.

4.

As I drink with high school classmates in the months before boot camp, and before I myself go to war, Antek, forty-five now, still dreams in some hazy way of escaping to the sea. Finally, after years of waiting, employment news comes in 1964. Struggling to catch his breath, he sits down to read the letter:

> Immediate employment available on Military Sea Transportation Service (Pacific Area) civilian-manned ships for the following: Third officers, junior deck officers, first, second, and third assistant engineers, licensed junior engineers, able seamen, oilers, firemen/water-tenders, and electricians.

Still up on the workings of the triple expansion reciprocating steam engine of the Liberty Ship, the EC-2, and on the Fairbanks-Morse trunk piston and crosshead-type engine of diesel-powered vessels, Antek has an opportunity to work in the engine room of a ship that will carry me to Okinawa, last exit before Vietnam. He could be responsible for the engine room machinery that guides his son across the Pacific. But instead Antek gives up on the policy of dreams that by now is reaching maturity and lets me proceed alone into the Tropic of Cancer. With his rapidly deteriorating health, there is no return to the seas of youth for my father. The man without a future grows bitter; his strength and talent haven't been recognized. He resents Mother and me. We've interfered with his plans for too many years.

I think about him as I cross the International Date Line. I think of him as thirty-five hundred Marines on many different ships steam south and east from the Ryukyus Islands into the heart of darkness. Twenty years later on a television screen in my parents' house I will discover what's lodged in my bleak heart.

EDDIE DABROWSKI'S PART IN THE WORLD AT WAR

5.

Now on a winter's day Antek sees an illusion amid the snow wisps the wind blows from the trees and the rooftops.

"Who's that?" he asks my mother.

I stand at the door in a snow-covered forest green military overcoat, which Ma calls a "greatcoat" in Polish. It has red chevrons on the sleeves. Beneath the heavy coat over one breast pocket of a uniform are pinned Vietnam Service, Armed Forces Expeditionary, and Good Conduct ribbons, below these a rifle sharpshooter's medal. When Antek looks closely he sees in the snow image a disturbing, long-ago memory of another man home from war. Looking again, he sees only the broken reflection of a twenty-two-year-old. Through his daydreaming, I've come home in a snowstorm. I stare back at him from inside a broken mirror, from behind a crooked photo. On the ID card you can see the crease start right above my service number, 2109925, where the lamination got wrinkled on the day of my discharge.

Now we tell each other stories. Father and son, two vets, we say to each other in Polish *"dawno temu . . .* once upon a time." After repeating the phrase so often, I grow interested in the minutes of long ago, knowing sadly that when he is fifty-seven, I'll be twenty-seven, when he's sixty, I'll be thirty, then on into the darkness of the times ahead, knowing, too, that as I pursue him into the future, he'll pursue me into the past. Now time becomes important. Living with my parents in Superior, Wisconsin, I begin to collect timepieces. In my room are a Sessions wall clock, a Westclox Baby Ben with two alarms, a Sunbeam with a lighted dial to shine the way—these and a few other watches and clocks, all of them wound and running.

"Why you don't study time for a living?" he asks.

6.

After watch repair technician's school, I work in St. Paul at a store on Snelling Avenue. Spending so many hours a day hearing time slow down, I decide to seek other opportunities the way Antek did. I return to his house where nothing's changed since the war in the Atlantic, where little has changed in the neighborhood, where the old days hover and there can be no way past them.

"Something got you down?" he asks.

Out of breath, he's sitting in his recliner, the weekly *Gwiazda Polarna* newspaper on the floor beside him.

"I don't think the watch repair game's for me, Pa."

"Time let you down like it did me then, hey?" he says, chuckling.

"I could try something. Maybe be night watchman on the docks."

"That's not no good for my son. You don't sleep away your night as a watchman. You go one station to another with a time key. Boss check on you. You go to this little box you open and call in to let them know you making your rounds. It's no work for you I don't think so. Why you don't do what you're trained for?"

"What am I trained for?"

"For working with time. Hold it in your hands, know what to do with it, see how it's robbed from you. Go back to watch repair this minute and be grateful you have the work."

"It don't suit me," I tell him. "Can't I just stay here with you and Ma?"

It's 1972 when I ask. In '73 Antek's lungs get him. He retires from Fredericka Flour. In a photo the company takes, he holds a retirement present, a Lord Elgin wristwatch. Now finally he has time on his hands. The instruction card that comes with the watch reads, "You can be confident your new Lord Elgin will stand up under the stress of normal wear. It has a Shock Resistant Guarantee." But it doesn't guarantee against shocks I bring Antek by drinking, by marrying the wrong women, by losing job after job in '75, '76, '77.

Living at home again, divorced, I've reached my limit by 1984. I want to clear socks, underwear, and old *Playboys* out of my drawers and leave the East End of Superior, Wisconsin, forever when Ma comes in holding the broken stem of her Wittnauer Geneva. Seeing her with the broken watch makes me want to cry and hold her. What does it mean when the precious stem breaks between mother and son and when hanging from a thin black shoestring in the basement is my father's pocket watch, the broken face never repaired? Has the time wound down an old family in a declining neighborhood?

Declining myself, I stay on with them.

7.

Antek's birthday. 1985.

Victory at Sea is in the videotape collection at the library plus an eight-part documentary on Vietnam. I check out three tapes then head to the Warsaw Tavern and Heartbreak Hotel for before-dinner cocktails.

"Where's Birthday Boy?" I ask when I come home for Ma's round steak and dumplings supper.

"Napping, Eddie," Ma says. "Be good to him."

He looks rough when he shuffles in, like he hasn't slept in two days, slippers dragging on the carpet.

"How's everything?" I ask, toasting him with a bottle of beer.

"*Dobrze.*"

"Sometimes there's not enough air for him," Ma says.

"Yeah, the air's heavy today," I say. I grab another one, pop it open. "Have one yourself, Pa."

He shakes his head no. He needs to conserve air by not talking.

After supper, after birthday cake, after he takes a shift on a machine he calls the "whoofer" and which he breathes from to break up what he calls the "glue" or the "butterscotch" in his lungs, I get out the video-tape about Vietnam, thinking I'll watch a little then get drunker and drunker in honor of his birthday.

We're sitting around the living room, Antek and Ma on the green couch when I put it in. These are *my* war years, not Antek's. "LBJ Goes to War" is printed on the videotape's plastic case.

"It's no war," Antek says right away. "Let's watch the other ones you brought home."

"Antek, quiet!" Ma says. "We watched *Victory at Sea* in the '50s."

"That was a war. A victory on sea and land."

"Pa, I spent time in Vietnam. I'm just understanding what went on. This is the first TV series made on it. Eat your birthday cake and quiet down."

"It's important to Eddie," Ma says.

When I start the VCR, the title comes up on the screen: "Part Three. LBJ Goes to War: 1964–65." We see green rice paddies. The water reflects the sunlight and ripples in the breeze. We see Vietnamese peasants running along the dikes, splashing through rice shoots and sunny water as they head for the safety of the bamboo woods. We hear a helicopter first, then see it on the screen. I hunch forward, sitting cross-legged the way Antek did in the old days when convoys appeared in *Victory at Sea.*

Now we see a soldier, an airman, shooting out the open door of the helicopter. The gunship swoops forward. The pilot radios back to the gunner, "Saw you splinter one right in the back with a rocket. Good job."

"*Głupiec* . . . Blockhead," my father calls the helicopter gunner.

Ma asks if I'll want dessert again later.

"No more eating. C'mon," I say.

I turn back, hunching so I swear I'm curled in half before every wristwatch I've ever fixed. Like Antek, split-faced, I've looked for myself in books, in movies like *Apocalypse Now* and *Full Metal Jacket.* This is live action on the television screen at Dabrowski's, live tragedy.

The destroyers *Maddux* and *Turner Joy* are steaming off the coast of North Vietnam in the video. The narrator is saying that on August 2, 1964, three North Vietnamese patrol boats attacked them. "President Johnson calls it an outrage. He promises we'll 'redouble our commitment to South Vietnam.'" Congress is passing the Tonkin Gulf Resolution. McNamara is barnstorming South Vietnam. A coup attempt is occurring in February in Saigon. "I went in March," I say.

Now in the video President Johnson is shown worrying about the unstable South Vietnamese government.

I'm saying to the birthday boy, "I'm gonna see myself, Papa."

"Turn away, Eddie."

Now bombs are dropping, their thunder heard on clear days.

"Turn away quick, Eddie," my father is saying.

"I'm gonna see myself, I swear it," I say and crouch lower in front of the TV.

General Westmoreland is calling for troops to protect the DaNang Airstrip. "The President," the narrator is saying on the documentary, "grants Westmoreland's request with little debate." I am saying, "Look how cloudy the tropical sky gets."

I know I'm there somewhere. I feel it. Something monstrous is going to come up on the TV screen. Time is going quickly. "Are you ready to land, Papa?"

Twenty years before. March. Gray skies, heavy surf, landing craft doors are opening, men in green charging out, wading ashore. "I'm seeing myself," I'm muttering. "There's me. See?" I'm whispering to myself, then asking him to look for me carefully and to please save me from what's going to happen. "What time is it?" I ask. My hair and forehead are wet from the humidity of the coastal lowlands. "Can you see me, Papa?" I say. "On March 8, 1965," the video's narrator is saying, "thirty-five hundred Marines land to protect the airbase at DaNang." "*There's* me!" I'm saying. "There's your son, the one you two raised." Now I can't help myself and am crying in front of them, in front of Antek and Ma. What kind of shipmate am I?

Out of meanness and vindictiveness, he says, "It's wrong. It ain't a war. You were wrong to go. That was no war at all there. It was a 'police action.'"

"Shhh, let me watch. Don't talk," I say, tears in the eyes of a thirty-eight-year-old man.

We wade ashore, our company. We walk up the beach. I remember digging in on Red Beach II.

It sounds like someone is in the room with me now. Maybe it is my reflection in the living room mirror.

"There you are, Eddie," Antek teases me.

I make out a voice. I hear a clock tick . . . hear someone tap a foot against a couch. Maybe it's my reflection signaling me after all these years. How can I be certain someone isn't with me when I try to see myself thinking on Red Beach II, and someone is willing to talk to me now in the living room?

"Rewind it," says Antek. He holds his chest, catches his breath. I think he knows how serious this war suddenly has gotten. "Rewind it," he says.

"No rewind," I say.

"Rewind, Eddie," he's saying. "Don't feel so bad. I'll watch you come ashore, Eddie. I won't tease you about wetting your pants."

"No, I can't rewind," I tell him.

Antek is saying something's wrong with what's on the screen. "There you are, Eddie."

"Where? You can't see me. You're just saying that."

I push a button to rewind, set it going forward to see if he's right. We're wading ashore. We're repeating a tragic morning on the coast in 1965.

"There!" Antek says. "*There*, there's my kid!" He claims he sees me crying on screen right in front of them. Bewildered, I'm wondering why I can't see myself. Antek says it's twenty years ago and that a lieutenant is yelling at me to get going with it. Antek sees it all before the screen goes blank. I've pushed STOP.

"Rewind it," Antek says.

"No."

"Yes!" he says.

I do. It starts again. I'm in the living room. It's twenty years before, March 8, 1965, that Antek says he sees me on the screen, head bowed, crying, walking in a foot of water just at the right of the screen. I'm being shouldered out of the way by men in a big hurry. Says Antek, "You shoulda stood up for yourself more. Eddie, why didn't ya?"

Then Ma's saying she sees Antek's Eddie from the neighborhood too, the watch repairman, being pushed around as though he doesn't belong in that country, that she's raised too good a kid for that.

I still can't see myself, but I remember crying on the beach. What happened in my life off-camera from that second on was going to be marked by my bootprints on that land and by the deep hole I, Eddie, dug in the sand of that beach where I spent my first regretful night in Vietnam.

"You no good bum," now Antek is saying. "The war do this to you, make you no good bum?"

When my father sees me on the screen, it's like he sees himself, the other side of his face. This old, foolish, two-sided father with the wrinkle in his seaman's card sees his fears and they are so like mine. Now the time has come. Now we're brokenhearted. The faces of father and son don't join. Nowhere. No joining. The sides of our ID cards don't connect. Me with my videotapes, him with his "whoofer" machine, we drift from war to war this night of his seventy-fourth birthday looking at our wristwatches, but unaware of the time and of who we really are. Antek and Eddie. Two Dabrowskis. A Cold War between us.

"Rewind it, Eddie," he says.

"No, Papa," I say.

"Just once more, rewind it," he says. This time I do.

"There I am, Papa."

"There you are, Eddie-boy."

"There I am, Papa," I say.

Immigration and Naturalization

An immigration officer, I have tracked down illegal aliens on ocean freighters and intercepted contraband in cars and trucks crossing our borders. As a result of these serious matters, I, Lester Stupak (the INS name tag reads), have filed enough Forms I-1551 and N-400 to fill up the Federal Building in Superior, Wisconsin.

Now a difficult case arises: my wife's, whose immigration claim I can't process. All I can do is sit by her bed and hold her hand. We've agreed over the years what to do if one of us dies—and now look, my Grace is leaving for a country I know nothing about. Who are its consuls and vice consuls that I might call to arrange her comfort?

"Lester, help," she implores when she is clearheaded from her medication and when the pain has ceased. I fix her pillows, brush her folded hands with my fingers, touch her hair with my lips, wondering why, dear God, she should die now when we have been so happy. No prayer helps until, from a brown bottle, I pour her morphine into a plastic cup. When she's through drinking, I dab the corners of her mouth. With her at peace, I sit here wondering how you give up thirty-eight years together.

"What, Dear?" I hear her mutter.

"Nothing," I hear her answering herself a moment later.

"Tell me something I can get you. Just tell me what I can do to make it easier for you," I say to her.

Because she wants nothing, that is what I bring her—helplessness, nothing. I wish I could suffer for her, but God does not bless me this way. Her frightened, half-open eyes, pallid skin, and morphine-stained mouth; nothing, no more horrible nightmare can befall me. I watch our life diminish by day and hour. When I am at work, I call to ask the nurse, who stays with her daytimes, whether perhaps something miraculous hasn't occurred with my wife Grace.

"Nothing." I can hear Grace herself saying it over the telephone. "Nothing. Nothing at all."

"What? What did she say just now?" I ask.

"Nothing, Mr. Stupak. I'm sorry," the nurse says.

One evening as I pray for a miracle and over the telephone try to find a priest available to me, Grace whispers how she can't endure it anymore. More softly than my inquiries about a priest, she says, "get my medicine"; and when I've given the little larger dosage the doctor prescribes, she says, "I have to leave. Take me from here. You have to help me, Lester."

"I will. But rest. You're weak. We'll go when you're better. Do you want a priest? All the churches are closing."

In my anguish I pray to saints who can't help—to the Patron of Lost Causes, the Patron of Safe Voyages, the Patroness of Married Women. But a few days later before she returns to the painless dreams where she spends her time, she says it again, "You have to take me someplace far away." "I promise I will," I say. Her body is now so frail she seems made of feathers or string when I move her a little on the bed.

Over thirty-eight years, there have been miracles though, sure enough. When we were young and Catholic churches stood on every block of that city, one small miracle occurred in Milwaukee, I recall as I sit by her. Settled in our first house, I grew worried we'd be transferred. I told her, "I should quit Immigration and Naturalization."

"Where would we have to go if you took a transfer?"

"El Paso. We'd have to sell. I'm worried and can't sleep. I didn't want you alarmed. I should just go to college, and we can stay here."

"You've got your time in with the government you'd lose. But we'll do what's best and support each other." As I sat at the kitchen table, she'd rested her cheek on my head, I remember. "Don't worry. Sleep. We'll decide tomorrow. It'll work."

The worry and frustration she'd helped me through that time—*you did, Grace, you got me through;* this was a miracle. Who knows but in its secular way it wasn't as great as what had happened spiritually to St. Theresa of Avila or St. Stephen of Hungary? *As things turned out, we never made it to the dusty Southwest, did we, Grace?*

Other miracles blessed us, I think now. Every color and curve of her face—a miracle to me! Always. How can a person care so much for four decades? Then there are recent, occasional improvements in her health, miraculous improvements that bring the renewal of hope.

But now the slow, sad decline, now the worsening back and neck, now the frequent pleas for help—then no one but me in her room kissing her as I try to delay her passing. The miracle of her life, which was *my* passion in life, is so suddenly over I can't believe it, and I continue to comment to her on the possibility of miracles. But none comes.

When I call at the mortuary, there is no urn, no vase, no formality, just a little plastic box. I bring her home. This is a week after her death and after the short memorial service conducted by a lay person, finally, for no priest was available. *And so, really, the loss of my life, too. The loss of Lester's life with Grace.*

At the start of the new week, I go to the office, knowing there is immigration work to do. A Brazilian is waiting, seeking Form I-589 and information on what a *"notario,"* a lawyer, can and can't do. A Laotian with two children comes next to apply for the Family Unity Program. By eleven of the first day back after Grace's passing, I know I can barely finish the morning when in comes my partner, who's been to the waterfront.

A sailor has arrived on a foreign freighter, he tells us. Clean-shaven, wearing a blue jacket and dungarees, the sailor, still a boy, makes no sense when he talks. His hands shake as we empty his pockets, pat him down, then call a translator.

"*Anyone* understand him?" Anderson asks.

"The shipping agent from Guthrie-Hubner said they got a letter a week ago when the kid was at sea," the secretary says. "It's from his mother. Someone at Guthrie-Hubner opened it, translated it. They got him off ship, brought him in. He's sixteen."

"I go back," the sailor is saying. He asks Anderson and Wilson, "Do you speak Polish?" Then he prays. It is as if the sailor is writing prayers on the legal pad the secretary's given him. "I go back," he keeps saying, scribbling with a pencil. "You mail for me?" he asks me. The address is: Dorota Fierek at *ul. Zniwno* 16/2 Gdańsk, Poland. I place it in my pocket.

"He wants a taxi to ship," Anderson says.

"Oh no," says Wilson, "you can't go. Government police wait for you. You'll be arrested. You're a protestor. You can't return to the *Ziemia Białostocka*. She's sailing for Poland the day after."

"Yes, go to Poland," says the sailor, whose blond hair falls across his forehead. Black eyebrows above the tired eyes contrast with his hair and with the face flushed with sorrow and excitement. All over there have been strikes: textile workers, coal miners, shipyard workers. The kid has been seen marching. I try to get the sailor's crying out of my head. It sounds like crying in every INS office on our floor—Vietnamese, Cambodians—sounds like it in the halls, at the vending machines, in the lavatory. At the elevator, I remember the Pole's letter. I mail it, then forget what's happened.

Everywhere at home, however, I am reminded of the comings and goings of asylum seekers. From Grace's window, I see a harbor and western terminus of Lake Superior and the Great Lakes. Ocean freighters load wheat for the Soviet Union, flax for Greece, heavy equipment for Saudi Arabia, corn, sunflower seeds, cement, even scrap metal for South Korea. Grain and cement dust rise above the gray docks, the terminals, the city. Looking out, I am reminded of émigrés wishing to leave an old country and stay in a new one. Sailors, illegals, wander the docks at night, waiting for their ships to return so they will have friends to talk to. My wife Grace has gone, and I have no one to talk to. I think if I don't do something to find her, I'll have to sit here with my head on the kitchen table, not eating or sleeping until someone, until Grace, comes. At nine, at nightfall, afraid of myself alone in the house, I leave for a place I know.

On the docks the security guard at Harvest States Elevator lets me pass. I turn toward the harbor slip, park the car. Grain silos tower overhead. Back to back, two ocean ships can load simultaneously at each dock, though the docks are silent tonight. Above the silos' vent fans, seamen have painted *"Belle Etoile* 12/19/82," *"Senator* of Athens 3/4/85," "M/S [motor ship] *Baronia,"* and a new name, *"Ziemia Białostocka."* Records of a visit to a terminal.

In the middle of the night, a lake freighter glides by. "Do you remember, Grace, we were to fix the house when I retired?" I whisper. Thinking of her, I put my hand to my chest. As I do, I notice someone moving. There. Outside.

Turning on the headlights, I see another hand rise to another heart, see a sailor's blue jacket against the night. Frightened, he hurries out of view, leaving me to remember his anxious face in the dark as the rain starts, leaving me to recall how bleak and gray life has been for so long. When she got sick, the room turned gray, the sky turned gray. While I comforted her, it'd rained for two years, for three years, for a decade. She'd snatch at the air with curled hands, the result of the morphine. Sometimes when I asked, "Grace, what is it?", she'd say, "Nothing."

"We'll take trips we never took before. We'll fix the house nice," I whisper to her when I think I hear her crying. But outside there. Again.

Now a tapping on the passenger-side window. The rain on the glass washes away the face.

"Who is it?" I call through the window. "What do you want? Your ship's gone to another dock. You were to have stayed in a hotel."

Rain, the blue lights on the dash, the name and time of visits on a terminal.

He taps again.

Slowly, he unbuttons his shirt. His youthful hand is lost beneath the jacket and the shirt. Lonely at heart, he wants me to look through the window at him. He wants me to see his heart.

"I've lost someone," I whisper, as I place my hand to my chest. A whistle comes from off in the harbor. So often I've heard the ships. He has only himself here in America. He was to have stayed in a seaman's hotel.

I see him, now closer again, through the rain. I see the hand pressed to the bare heart. I run my fingers across the inside of the window to his heart. "What is it you want? I've lost someone. It's nighttime."

He can't understand. He's looking for asylum and will have to cross the border with me, the representative of INS. If he does, I will explain to him in the car in the shadow of the silos just what has happened here tonight and why he can't return home. A "Request for Asylum," a Form I-589—he will need this signed by the Agent-in-Charge.

"Please, *pleace*," he is saying, "give me a ride from the rain."

I place my hand to the window, hold my hand to the glass so close to him. Nearly touching his heart, I see now in the passenger side window that I have become an old man who has returned so many people to countries they've fled, sent them to nowhere, to nothing, have had this power. How thin the glass of a window. Somehow the face I see in the reflection of the car window has sunken over the years, presenting an odd collection of angles to asylum seekers who never knew how to look on the face of nothing. How often I've told good people that evidence for wanting to leave their home country was insufficient. They'd sit there fearfully, expectantly. When others asked, "Is it hard to remain in America?", I'd point to the government pamphlet that read: *YES.* THERE ARE NO QUICK AND EASY WAYS TO OBTAIN ASYLUM STATUS. Remembering those whom I've denied asylum over forty years has given me heart problems.

Now Grace has died, and I am crying as I look for her reflection in the car window. The INS agent reflected in the glass offers little consolation to the weary traveler looking to him for asylum. "Here," I say to the boy. "Here is your Form I-589. Your Request for Asylum." I try to present it to him, but there is no way to cross this border until I open the door and unlock my sad heart to him.

"Come in. Yes," I say to him.

When he sits down, we look at each other in the blue light. He's been to sea and, home again, I ask to hold him. "Come. Just for a time sit with me. Please," I say. I reach for his hand.

He desires this, too.

We hold each other, the Agent-in-Charge and the young seaman, and no one ever needs to know how it is to be so lonely that a man will want to hold a boy in his arms in a parked car on a rainy night, maybe kissing him on the forehead before sending him out again onto the sea of darkness we live in.

Private Tomaszewski

I hide till dark in the brush behind Auntie's house. Around six, the light comes on in the window. At seven, worried about leaving footprints in the snow, I hurry alongside the house, walk up on the porch, and ring the bell.

When I'm back a few hours, my aunt fixes a place for me in the basement, where I read in the paper how a wild boar has gotten loose at the packing plant. "Interesting," I say as she inflates my old plastic swimming pool, mixes some water and a few bags of potting soil, and lets me roll around in it. Before I come back upstairs, she has to rub me down. The next day she calls for help.

"Psychiatrists don't make house calls," a secretary tells her. "Bring your nephew in if he's so sick as you say."

"I can't bring him," Frannie says. "He'll dirty up your office."

"Try the veterans' clinic."

She does.

"Sounds crazy to me," the doctor says when he comes over. An older guy, the shrink compliments me for serving in the war. "Korea wasn't popular, but we never got the insults you're getting."

Frannie brings him coffee. He sits in the living room, stares out at the park.

I'm on a rug in the corner.

"So you think you're not who you are," he says.

"What do you see?" I ask.

"Maybe I see a confused boy. Were you at Dong Ho, Hue, Saigon?"

Frannie gets up to excuse herself.

"No, Missus Mylok, you stay," says the doctor. "Your auntie sees a change in you, too," he says to me.

"It won't hurt telling him, Jerry," she says. "Now you two talk." She turns to the shrink. "He had no business being sent to Vietnam when his dad and ma are both gone and buried of natural causes. The military wasn't supposed to send him. He was living here with me. I'm the relative he's closest to."

"What about DaNang? That where you were?" asks the doctor. He lights a Camel. He smokes the whole cigarette, then notices the tobacco shred on his lip, which he savors on his tongue awhile.

"It rained all the time," I say. "We were outside DaNang about three miles, down below Division Ridge."

"He wrote home a lot, doctor," Frannie says. "He'd just put 'FREE' in the corner of the envelope. No stamps needed for our troops in Vietnam. I've got his letters where he says he's changing."

"I don't think we need them yet," he says. The doctor makes me feel good all of a sudden, like I can trust him, like he's said to me, "At ease, Private."

"We lived in 'strongback' tents with wood floors raised off the ground," I tell him. "Maybe twenty of us in a tent. We slept on canvas cots. In the middle of the night this guy Sergeant Hammerbeck got me up, told me to come outside. He was the new Platoon Sergeant who'd just arrived in country. 'What's wrong wit' you?' he asked me. It was raining. He had on his poncho. I don't want you hearing this, Auntie."

"Maybe we won't need you, Missus Mylok," the doctor says.

"I'll call your Auntie Ceil, tell her you're okay, you're doing fine. He's only just got home. The strain . . . The boy's tired. We all want him back healthy, doctor," she says.

"Care for a smoke?" asks the doctor. "You're entitled to GI schooling benefits, you know."

"I guess I've changed," I tell him. *It's just the doctor and me now.* "This Platoon Sergeant, Hammerbeck . . . I'd seen him in California. He was DI of a platoon there. Not mine, but another one in our training series at San Diego. In boot camp, we couldn't get packages or parcels from home, just letters. They wouldn't allow us to get what they call 'pogey-bait' in the mail—no candy, smokes, nothing like that. During mail call in boot camp, you slap letters with your hands. You run up and slap them between the palms of your hands from the drill instructor or you don't get your mail. This way you break whatever contraband's inside. Cynthia, my girlfriend, sent me a stick of chewing gum in a letter. I'd told her never do that. Gunnery Sergeant Welch must have felt the gum. He got me in the duty hut. Hammerbeck lounged in there.

"The Gunny made me chew the gum, the paper, and the foil wrapper. I stood in front of his desk. He said 'Swallow!' I couldn't do it. 'Swallow!' Gunny Welch hollered. I tried.

"When Gunny Welch got called out suddenly for something, Hammerbeck came up beside me. He whispered to me. We were in the duty hut. He was the drill instructor of another platoon. 'What's wrong wit' you, Private?' he said. 'Why d'you keep doing me this way? You know, I wanted you to have the gum. Here,' he whispered. He wanted me to spit it out in his hand. He went over by the file cabinet where he'd been lounging. He had on a campaign hat. He held a swagger stick. He chewed the Wrigley's Doublemint I'd been chewing."

"Your Auntie won't hear this," the doc says. "It's confidential between us."

"What is?" I ask.

"What he did or said to you."

"Well you can see what he did. He 'doubled my pleasure.'"

The doctor taps a Camel against our picture window. Frannie asks from the kitchen if she can come back in.

"Is Ceil home?" I call out to her.

"Yes. If you and the doctor like, I'll fix you both something to eat."

"Not for me," I tell her.

She calls back in: "Jerry?"

"Yes, Missus Mylok," the doctor says before I can answer again. "I'll have something to eat."

"That boar's still loose," Frannie says. "It got out at the packing plant. The stockyard said because of crossbreeding it's not dangerous anymore. Jerry. . . Doctor?"

"I'm getting to the pig part," I say.

Frannie comes in, sits on the green couch. The wall mirror behind her head shows how gray she's become. She wrote and sent me packages on my nineteenth birthday.

Doctor Oster crumples an empty cigarette package, gets a fresh pack from the coat in the hallway.

"My husband smoked Luckies," she says.

"I've been on Camels since the war," he says. "In Korea I would've walked a mile for a Camel."

"The 'smoking lamp' is lit, doc," I say.

"Jerry's *home*," Frannie exults as though she can't believe I'm here. I sometimes call her *Cioci* Frannie in Polish.

"It was always the boredom that got me," says the doctor. "Was it that way with you too, son? 'Hurry up and wait' all the time, hey?"

"I was so worried," Frannie says. "They crossbred out the wild part, thank heavens."

"Sergeant Hammerbeck . . . he said that he just wanted the best for me, that's why the gum," I tell the doctor.

"Let me be of help to you, son," Frannie says. She fidgets with the couch cover. The doctor leans forward.

"You know anything about the Marine Corps?" I ask.

"Jerry, son," Aunt Frannie says, "you had the phonograph record of 'The Making of a Marine' before you went in. He listened to it night and day, you know, doctor," she says. "Boot training."

"What do you know about the Marine Corps, doctor? I used to see guys doing chin-ups. They had to hang from steel bars and keep hanging or else. The DIs would grab you where you don't want to be grabbed if you came down without giving them enough chin-ups. It's a vulnerable way when somebody's got you between the legs.

"Anyway, I was sent over. We left on a MATS ship in December during typhoon weather. Broadway Street pier in San Diego to Honolulu to Yokohama. Then I went to Okinawa where I hocked my girlfriend's family's camera. I went back and forth from there to Hong Kong. We had to darken ship off of the China mainland . . . like everything was narrowing in on us. The earth and sea were changing, I know that much. All those changes, all that distance and the months I'd been away on Okinawa already. Then Vietnam. I was in DaNang quite awhile when I saw him walking into the compound, I don't know, like he was destined to. He knew me right off. He waited a month. Then that night when he called me out he was really crazy.

" 'I think that letter wit' the gum back in San Diego was meant for me, your Sergeant Hammerbeck,' he said. 'What's wrong wit' you anyway, Private?'

"I guess I don't want to talk about it, doc," I say. "I'd never seen anyone act like that. I'm gonna see who's around outside. He was really creepy. He was chewing gum."

"It's safe to go out for a while, Jerry," Frannie says.

"Sit down, son," the doctor says, "don't go out."

"Do you want me to tell you more? Hammerbeck waited a week to see me again. I'd feel his breath. I always knew he was around."

"He must've been in one too many wars," says the doc. "What was wrong with him?"

"Sergeant Hammerbeck saw something wrong in *me!* That was the problem. It corresponded to something wrong in him. I'd been in DaNang over four months. That means he rotated four months *after* me, rotated from the States to Okinawa, then to Vietnam four months later. I was gone from San Diego and four months ahead of him."

"You'd already been on Okinawa," says the doctor. "Four months."

"That's what I told you. Then he got there after me. He went to Koza and B.C. Street on Okinawa. He even made it to the same gook pawnshop where my girlfriend's family's camera was sitting on a shelf. How in hell? I mean he'd go to that particular one, that pawn shop, and to that camera out of all of them four months after I'd been there. Hammerbeck told me this outside my tent. 'Exposures remain on the roll you left in,' he said. 'Will I be better off starting fresh?' he asked. 'Is there any hope in the old roll of film, any hope of its turning out for us? The picture of us?'

" 'No,' I said. 'There is no picture of us.'

"He didn't like that. One day he had the pictures developed at the DaNang air base. He showed me them—two pictures were of my girl-friend. 'This the one who sent the gum?' he asked.

" 'Yeah,' I said.

" 'I'm tired of you fucking up, Private,' he said.

" 'What did I do?' I asked him.

" 'What did you do?' asked Sergeant Hammerbeck. He was an NCO. I was a Private. He made me do push-ups, made me say some-thing when I came to full extension of my arms. I went up and down in the push-up position, and after each repetition, I had to say what he ordered me to say. He watched and cursed, then went back into his tent to listen to me say it through the flap. 'I am an animal . . . twenty-one,' I had to say and count each new push-up. 'I am an animal . . . twenty-two,' I had to say. Spit hung from my mouth. I was wet all over . . . 'Thirty-nine,' I said. I was becoming something I didn't like. My voice got lower. 'Forty-one.'

" 'Louder! Keep at it!' he hollered through the tent flap. 'You stole my love letter, my Wrigley's Doublemint.'

"I'd lost pride, doc. I was dirty. 'I am an animal . . . sixty,' I said. 'I am an animal . . . seventy-two. I am an animal,' I said from the push-up position. 'Ninety-three.'

"Hammerbeck came out of his tent and saw the pig rooting with his snout. 'I am an animal,' I told him as though it would explain what I was doing. The place looked deserted under the floodlights that night. The power generators hummed. 'What went wrong with Jerry Tomaszewski?' the guys asked one another. When they weren't looking, I would check to feel the bristles along my spine, sharp like pickers."

"You're my nephew," says Aunt Frannie. "We see a troubled boy. You've got to get hold now that you're home."

"How'd we do in basketball? We beat St. Mary's this season?"

"We did," she says. "We lost to them, too, but we beat Duluth Denfeld for once."

"Both fans, hey?" asks the doctor. "I had a kid played a few years back. Your aunt says you went to Superior East—"

"My canvas cot was in one corner of this twenty-man tent," I tell him. "We had the sides rolled up all around because of the heat. I was way over in a corner. One night I heard someone breathing. I heard this snuffing sound in the dirt. When I put out my hand, I felt these . . . bristles. 'You steal my love,' he said. 'I want my gum. It was meant for me.' Mud clotted to his sides like it did to mine. I've been reading and studying about things. Look, Bradley M. Patten, *Embryology of the Pig*. 'The periodic recurrence of times when the mating impulse becomes the dominating factor in the reactions of an animal has long excited comment and conjecture. . . .' Look here, doc. 'A brief period of pronounced mating activity, when it occurs in males, is known to animal breeders as their 'rutting season. . . .' He had forty-four teeth."

"If you persist in this fantasy," says Doctor Oster, "you're going to make me smoke another pack of Camels." He was dressed in a suit. He smiled. His teeth were stained.

"One day after all of this . . . it was close to evening, he told us to move out. We went out Highway 1 across some rice paddies. F-4 Phantoms took off from the air base. They'd hit the end of the runway at DaNang and go up fast to avoid incoming fire. Here I was a pig, and I'm running, trotting right in there with the men. Nobody else saw Hammerbeck's hoofprints, his pig prints in the mud. You know, doc, once behind the tent in the dark, he called me a 'love-stealer.' What'd he mean by it? I never took anything from him. He was jealous of everything I did."

"I would say he needed help."

"Doc, we hit this path that went by some gook shacks and this place we called 'Dogpatch.' We went by some water buffaloes, some kids roasting a dog. We waved at the ARVN office, the Army of the Republic of Vietnam, and kept going out of town. Jesus Christ, I'm turning into a pig, I thought. I was rooting around in the mud and sticks when they weren't watching. I was scratching the dirt, blowing at it with my snout. Filthy with mud and happy, I grunted and kept pulling weeds. 'I am an animal . . . eight hundred and ninety-eight,' I said. They surprised us on the other side. The VC looked like me with their tusks. We opened up on them."

"Jerry, no more talk," says Frannie.

Doctor Oster crumples a cigarette package. "It's three packs," the doctor says. He keeps staring out the window. "Got any gum?"

"I was in the back of the line, it was dark, something sharp cut me," I say. "Auntie, I was frightened. I knew I was bleeding. I kept thinking how I'd like for us to beat Duluth Denfeld twice in a season, just once I'd like it to happen. 'What's back there?' someone was saying. Hammerbeck turned, I saw him turn. 'Nothing . . . it's nothing more than a pig. It's Private Tomaszewski,' he said. *He*, Hammerbeck, wasn't a pig then. He'd changed back into Sergeant Hammerbeck, USMC. I was the one doing the squealing, doctor."

"Oh, dear," Frannie says.

"I pushed off my hind legs the way you taught me never to give up, Frannie. I stood up on all fours. I squealed. My snout was ripped open, one hoof torn apart. I'd stepped on a mine. Everyone was stunned to see me standing in the full moon. Nobody fired. Flares went off. Whoever shot the flares up wanted to see if what they thought they saw was really out there. I could hear VC draw their breath. Even they were shocked. I couldn't locate the moon it was so bright out in the flare-light. It looked like we were in this big meadow of flowers I wanted to eat, and some I trampled. I went back and forth through the meadow with my hoof-slippers kicking dust. It was like a dance in the flowers by a pig. Everyone loved me.

"On the way in the next morning, my hoof and snout sewn back together, I was still too tired to laugh or talk. 'You son-of-a-bitch,' they said. 'You had us fooled. Whyn't you ever tell us you were really a pig, Tomaszewski?'

"'Afraid, I guess,' I said."

"Son!" Auntie says.

"They threw me mess-hall scraps. I got a Purple Heart. I think it was for the wounds as much as the flower dance everyone loved.

"In airports on the way home so many people stared that I'd grunt, squeal, and run through the hallways. I'd put in quarters and sit in private stalls in the men's rooms. I took a week getting here, some of it through the woods. It's funny how things like this transformation happen. I returned different. I mean, guys were changing. We even had a defector, an American who turned Viet Cong."

"How does the house look?" Frannie asks.

I stand up to look around. Balancing my two front hooves on the back of the couch, I stare into the mirror. "Look at how the tusks grow!"

Frannie stands up. Doctor Oster puts down his Camel. "It's good reality therapy," he says. "Your auntie and I see a fair complexion, sandy hair in the mirror."

"Look at the graduation picture on the table while I look in the mirror," I say. "I'm Jerry. I played basketball at East High."

The doctor stands by the stereo console. His cigarette smolders in the ashtray. Looking in the mirror, I see a large pig and two humans—Aunt Frannie Mylok and the doctor. Between the pointed ears, large hairs cover my snout. Since the medics stitched me up, the scars run almost to the ear on one side.

"I wish I looked better. What'll Cynthia think? She loves me."

Frannie runs her fingers over my face. "Look now, son," she says, "look here. Your eyes . . . your hair hangs down over your forehead just like in the picture. See where my fingers touch your eyebrows? There's nothing, not a thing wrong with your face. See your nose, your nostrils. Your mouth and chin are just fine. You look OK, no scars anywhere. You're the same as at school graduation from Superior East High. Your Auntie Ceil is okay, everybody else is too and wants to see you. No pig talk. It's having you back that makes us happy. We're all so happy."

A squeal rolls from my throat.

"I missed you, Auntie. The day I left—"

She soothes me. I start to cry. "How did this ever happen?" I say. "Some guys change. Things happen. I know you, Aunt Frannie, you and Uncle Frank, Dad and Ma and Grandma—you're all innocent. The government ran security checks on me. They gave me a security clearance to handle classified documents, confidential and secret documents. Don't you think they'd have known if something like this was gonna happen? I mean there's nothing in our history. Some things like tusks happen on you over there. When we crossed the ocean, the whole smell of things seemed way off somehow. Hammerbeck was covering up my way back home. I think it's a conspiracy to make us pigs. Hammerbeck wasn't even on ship with me and look what he did to me. He had this power. Look now, I remember what this book on pigs said: 'Sows failing to become pregnant will "come in heat" again after an interval of about 21 days, and maintain such a cycle until it is interrupted by pregnancy . . .'"

"It's no reflection on you, Jerry son, and you've got no scars that I can see," Frannie says.

"You know you can take so much." The tears on one side of my face roll down the street of scars to the tusk. I raise off my haunches. "It's warmer in the basement. I won't hurt anything there, not when I'm sleeping under the workbench. They gave me rabies shots. I'm not the same. You can feed me table scraps."

The doc stares and stares. He denies he hears me squealing. "I can't see any scars," he says, "just mental ones. It's hard, son. Emotionally and psychologically it's hard. I was in Korea, don't forget. Maybe . . . I don't know, it's why I smoke, I guess. Good thing I never started something more serious. But, you know, I don't care much for alcohol. That's a blessing, I suppose." He turns to Frannie and says, "Missus Mylok, we've got to start pulling your nephew back together, getting him to where he belongs. He's got his schooling to think of—Superior State College—and we'll see if we can't get him other benefits. But first we're going to have to spend more time talking. He's okay physically. He looks fine . . ."

"I've got a flaw, doc," I say.

"Quiet, son," he says. "You're okay. A normal American boy."

"I used to get classified messages. I'd bring them to Captain Nicoli or to the Warrant Officer. It was my job," I tell Frannie. "All kinds of messages would come in about a pig that'd been spotted in the rice paddies at night. They didn't know I was who the messages were about, that *I* was the message."

I raise my delicate weight off the couch. On all fours I walk past the doc, break into a trot around the living room. "I'll call for help," he says. "We've got to watch out. You're so heavy and big—" He dials a number.

"I'm going out," I say.

As soon as I leave, I hear the packing plant workers down the street. They've got a cage. They're still out looking for the boar that escaped.

It's like if you rotate back to the States, they'll get you. I roll around the porch, thinking about the neighbors and where I can hide—Kuzminski's house . . . Mataczynski's?

"Look!" one of them yells. "It's another pig's gotten loose over there!"

"Where'd it come from?" ask the other workers.

"Get him in the truck, Ralph!"

"Sure thing, Bill! Watch it now! Boy, if he ain't clever."

My hooves clatter over the pavement.

"Hee-ah! C'mon now, *Swinia*. Polish pig-swine!"

I show my tusks. I squeal and skip around.

"Hee-o . . . pig!"

They slam open the gate on the truck.

"Throw him in back!"

"C'mon there now, Mr. Pig, it ain't gonna hurt."

All the way down to the bay where the packing plant stands next to Fredericka Flour, I holler, "I've got a Purple Heart. I've got a Purple Heart! I'm a vet. I served Mass at St. Adalbert's, went to East High. My girlfriend's Cynthia Owstrowski. I'm no *swinia*."

"Don't bother with that pig talk. We won't understand you," they say.

I hear the squealing from down around the packing plant, boars and sows milling about, grunting, squealing. I see the big, scarlet FRED-ERICKA FLOUR sign.

"Thinks he went to East High School in the 'Friendly East End.' Why, I'm glad *I* went to Central High uptown. What about that?"

"He damn near beats all."

From in the truck I see my grade school, Saint Adalbert's. Sister Benitia is working late on the second floor. Sister Benitia is probably thinking she's going to teach her seventh-graders the miracle of what limbo is or of what the Trinity is or of how, during Mass, something as simple as bread and wine can be transformed into the Body and Blood of Jesus Christ. Now I am praying the Eucharist Prayer, saying it as a last resort, screaming it and squealing as loud as I can, "May the Body of our Lord Jesus Christ preserve my soul unto life everlasting." I am squealing, "Behold the Lamb of God, behold Him Who takes away the sins of the world." I squeal, but all I get in return are squeals.

The Wood of Such Trees

1.

Forty years ago, Hubba LaValley told me something about Satan. A sixth-grader, Hub was supposed to serve for an early morning weekday Mass at St. Francis Xavier, one of two Catholic churches in our neighborhood, but when he got there, it was pitch black inside. "I was reaching for a light in the sacristy," he said, "and I heard moaning. Father Matthew was always teaching us, 'Satan will do this to you. Satan will do that harm to you' and talking about the devil. Half asleep," Hub said, "I go up to the sanctuary. In the dark there's Father Matthew on a kneeler, drunk, a wine bottle by him. '*He* is among us,' he's saying. *Who* is, the devil or God? I was wondering when suddenly my eyes shot open! It's all I needed to hear at 5:30 in the morning. I got out of there. 'Wait!' Father was shouting. 'Come back.' I heard the wine bottle roll down the sanctuary steps."

The week Hubba told me this I thought about the devil nonstop. Four decades later, I'm still thinking about Satan. He makes sense to me now. I've seen what he can do. "Satan," the catechism taught us, "is a chained dog that barks furiously." The nuns back then said if we were wasteful and didn't fill both sides of a sheet of writing paper, then the devil would burn us to a crisp on it. Today, near the end of a century, I use both sides of paper before I discard it. At home my grandfather always talked about the devil, too. Then I suddenly began to see connections between the devil and my father, who was a kind of winter- or ice-demon whose mood corresponded to temperatures. When it was twelve below zero, the old man took it out on me, saying mean things or poking my arm. Roughing up your son—*that* was the devil's work. When it was fifteen or twenty below, I avoided the old man altogether. When he came home after work, I stayed in my room till the temperature rose above zero. A chart my father gave his customers read: "Approximately 50% of the season's coal requirement is normally used after January 15th, and approximately 10% after April 1st." Since it was probably late November when Hubba told me about Satan, I knew it'd be a long winter for me and my father, who delivered coal for The Hanna Company.

In Poland my grandfather worked in coal, too, though I saw no connection between the devil and *Dzia-Dzia*. Years after he and Grandmother arrived here in Superior, Wisconsin, with my father when he was a boy, coal mines still operated in Rybnik, Gliwice, Katowice, and Walbrzych in Upper Silesia. In America Grandfather worked on the Reiss Coal Dock. Retired and widowed, *Dzia-Dzia* or *Dziaduś* (names for grandfather in Polish) lived with us. Remembrances of the Old Country hung from the walls of his room—a painting of Our Lady of Częstochowa, a picture of the Sacred Heart in thorns. Hanging pinned within a folded bedsheet in his closet was another reminder of Poland: his ceremonial trade uniform.

"Try on the uniform, *Dzia-Dzia*," I'd say when I was young.

"Don't pester," Mother'd say.

"'Tis not the gown adorns the man but the man the gown,'" Grandfather would say.

Not only miners but other workers wore trade uniforms on special occasions in Poland. In a box in the closet, I'd seen his black cloth hat.

A golden tassel hung from the top. In front, two crossed hammers were stitched in gold, with gold leaf spun around them. I remember the uniform's coal-black coat hanging in the closet, the velvet tunic collar with the crossed gold hammers on it. The coat was wool. So was the green sash over the shoulder. When he wore the uniform, the coat had hung from Grandfather's strong shoulders to below the knees. The high black boots, unused now, gathered a polish of dust in the corner.

My father, on the other hand, had one uniform, a coal-blackened work coat and overalls. Ten or twelve times a day he'd back up the truck, pull down the chute, and turn on the conveyor belt that led into Milczewski's or Stromko's coal bins. When he got home or stopped by *Szkoła Wojciecha* to bring the nuns a partridge or the eels he'd caught through the ice on the Left-Handed River, it looked like someone had drawn wrinkles on his face with ink, except it was coal dust the artist used. No soap and water could wash out the lines of Apex Pochahontas or Pennsylvania Anthracite. The colder and blacker the days and his face grew, the angrier he got with everything. As temperatures dropped, he had more deliveries to make. Tired, he grew susceptible to the devil, who, the Sisters taught us, came out of the earth, had horns, and brought his fire to mark you.

One night with the heating season in full swing, my old man got riled up. Above the line *"Na wschodzie świta prześliczna zorza, rumieni zboża, pszenicki, żyta,"* I'd written in fountain pen, "In the east lightens the beautiful dawn, reddening the corn, wheat and rye." We were studying the conjugation of verbs in school, a lot of memorizing and repetition, so I wrote the line as a memory aid, then translated another line, "As long as learn you will not, until then shun you will all pleasure . . . *Póki uczyć się nie będziesz, poty omijać cię będą wszystkie przyjemności."*

"You wreck school property?" he said when he saw me, his hands black against the page.

"It's an old school book. Really it don't matter, Pa."

"You don't do that," he said. "I'll give you book, Aloosh. Did you clean the clinkers out of the furnace? You'll burn up the grates, you. Get down the basement. Don't get dust on everythink."

My father's work clothes hung beneath the stairs. His workbench stood in one corner, Ma's wringer-washer in another, coal bin in another. To keep coal in, he'd put boards across the front of the bin, leaving an opening at the bottom where you shoveled from. When he turned the light off on me from upstairs, it was a sign I should hurry and not use too much electricity.

"Can't you turn it on, please?" I called up, swinging the furnace door open against the dark and cold. Inside roared the flames. The devil lived there and in the grates below the furnace, I kept thinking. The white ash was his cast-off skin. He was preparing a disguise for the world, doing what he could to hide the redness of his flaming skin and tail. He could disguise himself as anyone, we were told. And if you stared a long time in a mirror and were vain, *you* might even see him like our neighbor Mrs. Krzyzaniak did.

On my knees I reached into the furnace with this little shovel. Putting the clinkers and ashes in a scuttle, knowing what was coming when I went back upstairs, I reviewed the future tense of "to strike, *uderzyć.*" First person singular: *I* shall be struck. Second person singular: *You* shall be struck. Third person singular: *He, she, it* shall be struck. Finished in the basement, I was thinking of what Hubba told me when my father flicked the back of my head with his fingers as I walked past him. "It's for good measure," he said.

I remember *Dzia-Dzia* coming in for a slice of bread that time. My old man, an immigrant, couldn't get American things right. He always called it "whole of the wheat" bread. He said to Ma, "Dorotee, give *Dzia-Dzia* and the boy a slice of whole of the wheat." The coal man was happy when he was eating and thought he could make everything up with me at supper. For the hundredth time, he told us what happened at Confirmation a month before when—asked by the bishop, "Who made the moon shine in the sky?"—a kid named Krynski said,

"Mr. Schmiegel, Your Excellency, he makes the moonshine in his barn." Ma laughed at the story. *Dziaduś* did, too, but how much English did *he* really understand? I wondered. As Grandpa went back to daydreaming at the table, Joe Szczniewicz had a brandy and talked about the day's coal activities. Then we bowed and prayed.

"Here, Boy, eat," he said when Ma put out the fried potatoes and Polish baloney. He heaped a scoop of potatoes on my plate. "Mix up wit' the baloney," he said. He placed a piece of bread on top of it all. My father ate happily with his sleeves rolled up.

Later when Grandpa went to bed, the old man changed again, though. "You need improvement," he told me. "You have to take responsibility. What happens, you forget to clean the ashes?"

"The grates burn out, Pa. No heat."

"You want *Dzia-Dzia* sick, you?"

"No, sir."

"Ah, you kid," my father muttered, tired of the long, difficult hours of the coal hauler. Then Mother piped in, "Sister Benitia told us you want to be a priest."

"I'll give him priest," said my father.

In the coal season the devil was always close in a mirror or in a furnace, it seemed. I once even held a mirror up to the open furnace. All I saw was fire. The word for him in a dictionary is *djabeł* or *szatan*. I'd asked the nuns about becoming a priest because I guess I wanted to help the East End get rid of *djabeł*. Sometimes to get him off my mind he was there so often I repeated what the coal company chart read: "The lowest temperature ever recorded in Superior in any November was -29 degrees, in December -35, in January -41, February -36, March -26."

One day as the temperature dropped again I got to wondering whether *djabeł* had more control of me than I thought. I started pondering how far I'd go before betraying the old man. In 1957, nuns, grandparents, great-aunts, everyone in the world said Communist kids spied on their families in the Old Country. Sometimes the kids' parents were arrested by the secret police and sent to Siberia, and the kids became heroes for turning them in. Would I report the coal man if we lived in Poland or Bulgaria? Then I realized, before I fell asleep that night, that no matter what Joe Szczniewicz did at home, he was my father. I couldn't report him to the NKVD or ZOMO. I'd found peace from *djabeł* and his pomps and works, then went to sleep listening to the creaking of an old house in early winter.

Ma always called me in the morning, "Get up! Your father want you." I could see the cold, gray sky from bed. In the kitchen he would be stirring oatmeal, waiting for me. "Throw in a shovelful, you," he'd say. Then sometimes he'd tell me, "You come to school in truck when you finish the breakfast. I give you ride."

Risking my life and health, I'd tell him, "No tanks. I don't wan' no coal on me." I kissed Ma's cheek and *Dzia-Dzia's* white head that time and left. Passing St. Francis School, no doubt I'd seen Father Matthew wandering around outside, hands shaking from drinking, from seeing Satan, and from hearing his ferocious bark.

2.

At St. Adalbert's where the Polish people worshipped, kids laughed at the old people for saying, "Everythink no good in Poland no more" or "You study you school book, den you haf time go play." Other days we dozed until Father Nowak came onto the altar. Then the *babas'* prayers grew louder than a coal truck.

During Mass I'd look through my *Saint Pius X Missal* and dream. A red ribbon marked pages I still keep beside me as the century ends. In the back of the book, a "Table of Movable Feasts" told on what day feasts like Ash Wednesday and Easter were to be celebrated during the years right up to 1997. In 1957, Advent Season would begin in three days. In the next year, it would begin on December 3; the year after on December 2. The Table of Movable Feasts went from when I was thirteen years old to now when I am fifty-three and there are few churches left in Superior and the last one is closing in a month.

I remember wondering whether St. Adalbert's would be around in the years at the end of the Table of Movable Feasts or whether the Communists we were being warned about would have taken over by then, sending my parents in a boxcar to Siberia; me, Aloosh, to Moscow, where I'd be celebrated for turning them in. I thought Józef Stalin would be responsible, not Bishop Hammes, but that is not what has happened in Superior, Wisconsin: the bishop has closed our churches. No priests, he's said.

On the afternoon of that day in a November long ago, I called my father "*wrona*, crow" in front of my schoolmates. As the furnace would come on those evenings, I remember sometimes (maybe I'd gone to confession that day and had been thinking about things), I remember I regretted ever ridiculing him when he pulled up at school in the truck. I'd called him "*węglarz*, coal heaver" too, yet my father got up in the middle of the night to throw coal on the fire, went to work on days off if the company needed him, and did a lot for the nuns, especially Sister Benitia whom he always brought an eel to put over her heart when it acted up, an old custom from Poland. The warm air coming into my room traveled up through vents my father cleaned, too.

Then there'd be this counter-impulse, and I would think of the devil in the furnace. Ash gray, he'd start calling up to me through the vents, "Aloosh, betray your father. Give in to sin. Please. I am a chained dog. Let me free." I shut the damper.

3.

One day after school during some of the earliest days on the Table of Movable Feasts, I asked Ma, "Can I walk to the river?"

"Stay off the ice. You don't shoot at nothink with that .22. You know your father don't trust you shooting nothink."

"I'll keep it unloaded till I get down there," I told her.

Thinking back on it, what happened during that afternoon, or that week of my youth, seems insignificant compared to the sins of my later life. Still, I was haunted in those early days. I remember how the chained dog barking made me think of a man who was eaten by mice and of another who had worms in his teeth. Such were the thoughts of the devil. I thought of a picture I'd seen in a book. In the painting "The Punishment of Unfaithful Wives," King Bolesław the Bold is forcing the unfaithful wives of his soldiers to suckle dogs. When I heard the barking and snarling of the devil, I had other thoughts. He was chained to a tree by the river.

I'd shot empty cans before with the coal man, who hunted crows for bounty. I wouldn't shoot anything by myself, I'd promised Ma; but when I saw a rabbit crossing the ice, I couldn't help it. I shot twice. When I got to him the rabbit was on his side, jerking. I walked around him telling him what Krynski said to the bishop about moonshine, telling him about the man with worms. A light snow blessed the rabbit. He was a foot long. I didn't know where to put him, so I apologized to him. Piling snow over him, I made it look like he was covered up and sleeping. A crow in a birch tree flew off. Where would I go? I wondered. The .22 in a canvas case, I ran the mile straight to my father.

"Aloosh," he was saying from his company truck. "Why you come here? Let me dust myself off, get the lunch pail. Then we go home." Dust circled his eyes. In the coal yard, everything was black. The gray sun set as we walked up the road home. Seeing us, a guy yelled at Joe and me from the highway, "On'y way to kill two Polacks is to wash their feet!"

Tired, slouched over, Pa laughed, waved his lunch box. I laughed at the joke as I hurried along.

In my mind I'd mapped out the way home the way I do today, a visitor to the neighborhood forty years later. When I saw *Dzia-Dzia* that afternoon at the table and heard Ma asking Father, "How was your day?", I knew I was safe that time. I'd felt lost with Hub's talking about Satan, with the nun telling Ma about a vocation I wasn't sure I had, then with the rabbit and the guy yelling at us. Then, too, the lie made me think I had worms in my teeth.

We lived in a country of woods. I used to draw maps of the woods country all the time, putting in the swamp, the Left-Handed River, the birch trees that stood at the edge of a blue forest. I'd also put on the map the coal yard, Fredericka Flour, the packing plant, the Isolation Hospital. Guessing the heights and depths of hills and bays, I'd try to understand my father's heart from them.

Everything that had happened during that week around Advent was written somewhere else, too. It was on a map that would show Albin Szczniewicz (who one day finds himself roaming his neighborhood again): 1) imitating his father, 2) writing in his grammar book, 3) avoiding his furnace responsibilities, and 4) shooting a rabbit. On this other map—not of places but of the people and events of those times—would have been our priest Father Nowak, Sister Benitia, the school kids, the sick lady Hedda Borski who never left her house, the twins Freda and Greta Zielinski, the Table of Movable Feasts, *Dziaduś* in uniform, and many other things. This map that wasn't written down anywhere—it was a prayer doubling as a map.

That night in my room I remember reading fervently out of the missal, "Jesus, Joy of Angels." I imagined the neighborhood's nuns, bartenders, butchers, widowers, everyone, responding in voices of joy and anguish, "Have mercy on us."

"Jesus, Strength of Martyrs," I'd whispered.

"Have mercy on us," neighborhood people said in my imagination.

"Jesus, Light of Confessors."

"Have mercy on us."

"Deliver us."

"From all evil."

"Deliver us," I prayed again.

"From the snares of the devil."

So much went unnoticed in our old house and neighborhood. *Dzia-Dzia* in his room thinking of the miners of Silesia; how did you write him on a map, or how do you now—or the patterns in the wallpaper, the patches on the chairs, the linoleum curling at the edges of the kitchen floor? How would I write on a map that when I wanted to talk about the rabbit, my father brushed me away, saying, "You too smart with the mout'"? How can I write even now that our churches have closed and that I weep for how things have turned out?

Most of the time the distance between *Dzia-Dzia*, my father, and me was like the distance separating those days from these, which are perilous days when people have little to believe in.

That time, half asleep, I didn't hear Joe come into my room.

"Why've you got your work clothes on, Pa?" I'd asked, surprised.

"I got to go back. Come on. The furnace."

"I forgot," I'd probably said. "Otherwise I'd have done it, Pa."

"Come on."

I'd have hated going out like he had to back then. He wore the work coat, work shirt—the usual uniform.

"Pa, I have to tell you something," I'd said as we went to the basement. I remember this clearly, how hard it was to get out but how I had to then or never would.

He was saying how cold it was, like he wasn't listening, when I blurted it out. "I laugh at you for delivering coal, Pa. So do other kids. But I know I couldn't report you to NKVD or ZOMO if we lived in Poland." I wasn't sure what I was saying except I felt bad he had to go out and that so much had happened to me lately. I thought if I didn't tell him, my own father, how I called him "crow" and other things, *djabel* would isolate me from him, which was the devil's work—and then I would never be able to talk to him. "I shot a rabbit. I lied to Ma," I said to him. "You won't make me climb in the furnace, will you?"

When he smiled, his coal wrinkles eased a bit, and it was as if he wasn't angry at all. "Aloosh, we have Polish saying: 'What the father forgets, the son remembers,'" he told me. "You good son. I have no trouble with you. I see myself when I look at you."

I think now that he knew what I was talking about. It was a map he'd been on. I think he knew how I'd stuck up for him a few times in front of kids, too. The radio playing upstairs, the floor creaking as Ma walked to the sink, the chiming hallway clock, the smell of the whole of the wheat bread; this was a map of the feel of things in a simpler time. On the quiet shore nearby, the moon was shining as it was on us and on the trees where lay the dead rabbit I hoped God would bless.

In the basement, Joe Szczniewicz had opened the door to the furnace grates and grabbed the bucket.

"No, lemme."

"*Dziękuję*, Aloosh," he said. He put a shovelful of coal on the fire. Then we went back upstairs.

"You going to remember thees house when you fifty, sixty years old?" he was saying.

"I will," I said many years ago in a different life in a different country when churches were still open.

I left the ash pail on the stoop and walked him to the truck, I remember.

"What's the word for rabbit?" I'd asked.

"*Królik.*"

Then he surprised me. He put his rough hands to my face. I couldn't believe he could ever do something so gentle. "You don't worry about nothink," he said again. "Everythink always be all right for my boy."

I watched the coal truck drive away into the night, my father's stack of temperature charts on the seat beside him. Ma had turned on the porch light. *Dziaduś* was looking out the kitchen window at the trees of a moonlit neighborhood, the trees of the Old Country of East End Superior.

I dumped the ashes, walked back through the snow to the house.

"What time is it?"

"Eight o'clock. *Father Justin's Rosary Hour* on radio is just over," my ma said. Grandpa was playing a record on the *fonograph*, Ogiński's Polonaise "Farewell to My Country, *Pożegnanie Ojczyzny.*"

"Pa said for me not to worry about anything," I said in the kitchen as *Dziaduś* played the polonaise again.

"Here, you," *Dziaduś* said. He handed me a black cloth patch with crossed gold hammers he'd gotten from the sleeve of his ceremonial uniform. He'd taken out the stitches with a pair of scissors. "He's been at it all afternoon," Ma said.

"'Tis not the gown adorns the man,' *Dzia-Dzia* said, 'but the man the gown.'"

I put it in my room, I remember, with the scapular and holy cards from St. Adalbert's Church and *Szkoła Wojciecha,* our school. I thought that if someday I got lost, I would have the map of this Polish neighborhood to direct me back. I'd have rosaries, scapulars, and a prayer book with a Table of Movable Feasts I could pray from no matter where I was. I had a coal man's insignia, too, and now in the snow outside of the house where I was born, I am saying the litany, "Lord Have Mercy On Us . . . Christ Have Mercy On Us," for I was never so good in the ensuing years and have looked in mirrors and felt the worm of sin. And now I must study the map that has led me to a house someone else inhabits. *Dzia-Dzia* and my parents died long ago.

I've come three days of hard driving to stand in the dark remembering directions I've drawn of the past. Rivers are ice-covered tonight, the neighborhood quiet, though three bars and a market are open. No one knows I'm here. Not *Dzia-Dzia.* Not the coal man. The map has grown to include other states, the loss and the recovery of faith, the many new people who've found a place on it. It includes things I should never have done in life. Anger, hostility, the war in Vietnam, my narrow-mindedness, impurity, covetousness, the envy of others' success in mine, the map-maker's, trade.

But that is not the story to be told; for just as in 1957, I have also done what was right—been faithful in marriage, been honest with people, drunk moderately, given to charities. Everyone is a sinner, some greater than others: I have, I guess, been mediocre in this way. What *is* to be recalled is how the next morning back then I had to serve Mass. St. Sylvester, Abbot, whose feast day it was, founded an order of priests. On the way to church—it was a Saturday, I remember—I looked at the buildings of the East End neighborhood (so many torn down or abandoned now)—at the icehouse, at Stanski's Market, Kasuba's General Goods, Nadolski's Warsaw Tavern, the place where the Isolation Hospital once stood . . . at the birch trees along the avenues and in the yards, then down at the coal yard. I watched old women in woolen scarves and long overcoats hurry to church with rosaries and prayer books.

I probably daydreamed about Monday when Bernie Gunski and I would be doing something to aggravate the nun, when Bobby Kiszewski would be imitating Sister Benitia's broken English, and when Joe Novack would be counting on his fingers to get his arithmetic done. All of it the devil's work in little things.

"Ah, you. Hurry, Mass will begin," Benitia'd said back then. Leaning outside the church vestibule were four spruce trees to decorate the altar during Advent.

"You theenk about vocation, Szczniewicz?" the nun had asked as I'd followed her into the sacristy.

The *babas* murmured in their pews, nodding, blessing each other. They'd heard rumors of a budding vocation. "A priest someday! Look!" they were all saying and pointing to me, to Aloosh. Once Sister handed me the cassock and surplice to wear, I didn't have time to think about the future that was opening before me back in 1957, a future where, in many ways all these years later, the devil has lost his ferocious bark, but I have come home anyway to remember how it was when he was a greater presence in East End.

The Month That Brings Winter

Or, How Mr. Truzynski Carried Vietnam Home with Him

Mr. Truzynski of the East End of Superior was an army vet. In the shed behind his mother's house, which stood within sight of the old Pest-house, in this shed amid a rake, a shovel, and several onion and potato sacks filled with copies of *Life* and *Look* magazines, there hung a uniform with his ribbons and the rifle insignia. He would come out to the shed for one of his tools from work and find himself over where the shed wall had half fallen down. His back ached, and the cold came right up through his boots. But he was at home in the shed, and when he came into his mother's house and looked out from the kitchen, where he *should* have been comfortable, he knew he'd left part of himself hanging with the shovels, the sacks, and the old news of the Ho Chi Minh Trail and the DMZ.

Returning for the pail or the brush he'd forgotten—for Mr. Truzynski was a furnace cleaner before he went to Vietnam—he would think how he needed something in life before he, too, leaned so far over he caved in. On these visits to the shed, he dreamt of the monastic life. God was the answer, he thought, although it was as if God had withdrawn His blessed light when, these days in the northern latitudes, the sun rose at 7:52 A.M. and set at 4:23 P.M. Anyway, he was lucky to have a job and lucky to be back from the war, and the autumn passed quickly and the coal and furnace business picked up again, and it all caught fire for Mr. Truzynski.

On the shortest day of the year, five months after his return from the service, he found his automobile covered with a delicate morning frost. It sparkled in the streetlights and on the '56 Studebaker. "Vapor-bearing air," the weatherman had called it. Mr. Truzynski laid his equipment in the car trunk and placed his thermos on the front seat. Seven o'clock in the morning, no sun, black outside. This time of year things turned around on themselves from what they used to be. Night was long, especially when you worked in someone's basement all day. But if that was the job—, he thought. He looked at the shed behind his mother's house on East Fourth Street near the ore and coal docks. The frost lay like a velvet, seductive depression on the tarpaper walls.

The furnace man took Stinson Avenue to work. By the time he crossed the Tenth Street tracks, he was in a working mood. He liked the drive which took him past the creosote plant where the tar on railroad ties and telephone poles came from. On the railroad siding by the plant, he observed a string of tank cars. Tar vats exhaled steam. Buildings, railroad tracks, yard locomotives, even the air—everything was spattered or covered with tar. The creosote plant spewed tar fumes into the air and chemicals into a creek, which wound through the East End to the bay. Black ice formed on Newton Creek by the Pesthouse grounds, and kids came home stinking. The town—a harbor town on the deepest and coldest of the Great Lakes—needed desperately to keep out the tar. There were other problems with the city. Coal dust plagued it; it bloomed like wild, deadly flowers. You couldn't hang out your wash.

When the road went through the woods beyond the plant, the landscape changed. Out here there wasn't as much tar on things. Just the vapor-bearing air covered the trees with white this morning. He'd read in the paper that, during winter solstice, people up here dwelt in two-and-a-half more hours of darkness per day than those further south in Texas, say, or Mississippi. He thought of his uniform, of old *Look* and *Life* magazines hanging in the onion sacks during all that long winter's night; and it was as if history itself—for certainly there was history in the former sergeant's uniform and in those magazines—it was as if history had been temporarily blacked out and there was nothing happening in the universe, no history being made in the darkness.

He found a two-story building at 209 32nd Avenue East. In the fog he couldn't see the end of the rectangular building, an old store or boardinghouse, he thought. Tin covered the place. You could see where the carpenters or siders had begun to lay the tin, then stopped. You could count hundreds of strips of tin nailed against the sides, an ugly, hopeless color the dark, somber green of military fatigues. Each section had a quilted pattern. He'd never seen such tin covering a house or building. Fifteen windows ran along the upper floors.

"Mr. Truthinski, the furnace cleaner?" asked the two women who met him.

They'd been sipping tea and fidgeting with things as they waited, they said.

"No, it's Truzynski, Tomasz Truzynski. True-*zheen*-ski, emphasis on the second syllable in Polish."

"Mr. Truzynski, bring in your equipment."

Greta and Freda were identical. In their middle forties. Thin and pale. They must be sisters, he thought. As they extended their hands, long, thin fingers moved together. When Freda touched her mouth or her ear with a fingertip, so did Greta.

"It's dark," one of them said. The other switched on a light. "This helps . . . yes, uh-hum." They wore gloves and sweaters over their dresses. The door they took him through led to a hallway. Bent forward, the one who turned on the light hurried so fast she disappeared.

"Be careful, yes?" said the other. She pointed to the basement door.

"It's a bad time of year," he said.

They were nervous ladies. Sometimes they spoke in a strange tongue. Hungarian, no Rumanian, he thought (as if he knew). Right then, one pulled a scarf from her sweater. She tied it beneath the chin. He caught a glimpse of her gloves adjusting it before she turned her attention elsewhere. He could see the other again now.

"What sense in burning electricity?" one said. She found a switch and went down the wooden steps. "My name is Freda."

"Mine is Greta."

To Mr. Truzynski, the building looked to be very deep and long. *The shortest day of the year, no light, and I'm going into the basement.* It was like the quilted building had to give up something and decided light was less important than room and space, as if all the room on the upper floors and in the dark basement could offer strength against a short day with no sun.

"What are you thinking, Mr. Truzynski?" asked Freda.

"How I can't carry all my equipment myself," he said.

The wooden steps shook. He left the pails and brushes at the landing. Ducts and flues ran up from the basement through the first floor. He could see a few washstands and a cast iron sink in a corner. He couldn't see beyond them. There was twilight, then blackness in the basement. "Come in," one, or perhaps both, said when he got down there. "We're here a lot."

He looked up at the beams of the ceiling.

"There's something here," they said. Freda (he *thought* it was Freda) turned on a dim light. Motioning to him, she reached out, pulled open the furnace door. "Yes, uh-hum." She picked at the knot in the scarf, put her hand to her cheek. They did it together, synchronized.

He got more equipment. He saw the last of their crepe dresses go up the stairs. As he struggled into the furnace he heard their hard black heels on the floors above. Then silence. He shined a flashlight. There was no room to turn inside the furnace. Wherever he did, coal dust flew up.

He pulled a cap, goggles, and breathing mask from his pocket and went to work, being very careful of the furnace and of its various ducts.

When he was done, he ached all over. Covered with soot, his eyes and mouth irritated, nevertheless he was satisfied that no coal dust would soil the walls upstairs. He took great pride in his work. He wanted people satisfied with what he did for them. His mother had taught him pride in a job well done. He pitched the last of the equipment into the Studebaker. He looked at the quilted sides of the house. The second floor was all windows in a row. As he drove by, he thought he saw the sisters running from window to window. He'd been in the dark. All day it'd been night in the house, and in a few hours the sun would set. No one shut off furnaces to be cleaned in winter, he thought. Not wishing to smell the creosote, he took a different route home to his part of East End.

Tomasz Truzynski's dear mother was so particular about her house and about the sergeant that she wouldn't allow his uniform inside.

"Was it profitable today, Tomasz?" asked Mrs. Truzynski.

He nodded. "These sisters!"

Mother had supper ready.

"Yes?" she said.

"These twins . . . a furnace."

She served him sauerkraut, ribs, a boiled potato. "Do they have marriage in mind?"

"No," he said.

"Why, Tomasz, marriage is all right."

"Maybe I'll go out to the shed for a while, Ma. Visit my uniform," he said after supper. "I've got to go back to Greta and Freda's to finish up tomorrow."

He sat an hour. On a pail on the shed's cold dirt floor, he paged through *Look* and *Life*. Not only the cold but the dark got to him. Soon he had to forget himself and go back in.

"So what did you decide that you're thinking so deep?" his ma asked.

"I don't know," he said.

He went to his room, and after an hour, she came in.

"Tomasz?"

"It's not all of a sudden, Ma." He lay in clean clothes on the bed. "Ever since I've been home I'm in and out of furnaces. It's dark when I get done. I don't know. I hear it all the time through the vents. I go down in basements. I come up and it's always dark and I'm full of coal soot. I know it's honorable work, Ma, all work is, but it's not uplifting work really anymore. There . . . not uplifting. I've said it! I'm thinking about, well . . . becoming a priest."

She backed out.

His tired and sore back and shoulders were better the second day. He'd gone to bed early. Now he felt prepared for work again.

When they saw him coming through the corner of the window, they fidgeted with their cuffs. If he called her "Freda," she said "Greta." If he called Greta "Greta," she said, "No, Freda." He wondered at his mistake, wondered whether *anyone* could tell them apart.

They went down the hallway, but in a different direction. Greta and Freda wore scarves and gloves.

"Watch the steps, uh-hum. There's no light."

They entered the basement a different way. They hadn't said whether they were satisfied with their furnace cleaning. He felt the cement floor at the foot of the basement stairs. Greta, or was it Freda, he wondered, found a switch, turned it on, climbed down yet another flight of stairs deeper into the basement. "It's a big house. Plenty of space," she said. She looked at him. "There," she said: in the dim light, another furnace!

Mr. Truzynski believed vents and flues occupied their thoughts. Though he had his own flashlight, she left hers, Freda did . . . or Greta. The mask, goggles, and cap on, the brushes and pails ready beside him, he set to on the second furnace. They must be frozen stiff upstairs, he thought as he began brushing. He heard muffled voices through the ducts and vents, voices that must have traveled a long way down to him in the basement. Suddenly, though, the sisters sounded closer.

"You went without heat?" he could hear one ask.

"Yes, uh-hum," the other said.

"Yesterday you were Freda."

"No, Greta."

"I'm Freda!"

"Then who am I?" one of them asked.

It echoed so he heard it again and again: "Who am I?" Greta or Freda—he didn't know who the other was. He didn't know it wasn't Freda who paid him or it wasn't Greta who asked him to return.

In the five months he'd been back in business he'd cleaned nearly forty furnaces, and last week cleaned the furnace at the Heart and Flame Saloon in the "Friendly East End," as businesses in the neighborhood advertised themselves. The cleaner of furnaces gets to the heart of a house or business, cleaning ducts and flues in a way that, when the furnace goes on, no ash flies out. He carries off bucket upon bucket of the soot of winter's burning; and all this time climbing in and out of furnaces, he is careful of grates and linings.

When he did the Heart and Flame, which a year later would be called Heartbreak Hotel, what crying had come down through the vents. It happened week after week that he'd walk into a house or place of business and see its owners trying to stop crying or arguing. But it was no use and they knew it, and once he was in their basements, they'd start again. He'd crawl in and begin brushing when he'd hear things, hear sorrows, coming down through the vents, ducts, and flues. "Don't," a wife might be telling her husband, and Sergeant Truzynski, who really knew the truth, would hear the husband sobbing. By the time all the pails were full of dust and Mr. Truzynski himself was breathing it and his face was black, he'd hear more weeping. Surrounding him in the furnace, through every pipe . . . weeping. Sometimes his whispers rose back up through the arms of the house as though it were the Mekong River.

Now Greta and Freda waited for him. "Will you wash up?" they asked him. It was four o'clock.

"Yes, you'll wash up," they said.

Mr. Truzynski brought his pails up. It was near dark. He was losing sight of the sun.

"Sure I'll wash up. Lemme dump the equipment," he said.

When he got to the car, he realized he was missing a brush. He hoped he'd find it on the porch or in the hallway; but having no luck there, he had to climb down first one flight of stairs, then another. The furnace door hung open. He felt around the interior. No light—just the wary beam of Mr. Truzynski's flashlight roamed the furnace. At least he had plenty of space outside of the furnace. The basement—like the long, quilted house—went on and on into the earth. But what of all that space he couldn't see into? Did it make up for the lack of light in some way? he wondered. He had tried being prudent, but his job took him down stairs into basement secrets. When God canceled winter's light, when the darkness held sway over all, there would still be the space and void beneath East End Superior.

He thought to himself now: *Your water pipes will freeze up there if it gets real cold, Greta and Freda. You're going to have to start a fire. It's a sin to let your water pipes freeze in winter, Freda and Greta.* Then he thought again that he wanted to be a priest. *Then you can tell me your sins, Greta and Freda.*

They shut the damper on him. He heard it slam. He felt around for the wire brush, which he found in one of the ducts.

* * *

When he got home Mother said they'd called.

"What'd they want?"

"Just wanted you."

The phone rang as she said it. Army Sergeant Truzynski answered. "Yes?" he said. One spoke, but he could hear the identical twin behind. "You sound like you're in a furnace," he said to them. "Are you calling from a furnace?"

"We'd like to thank you for the work ('Hush, Greta!') and tell you to stop again. We're sorry we shut the damper," said Freda.

Mother said after supper, "They're soft on you."

"Oh, I suppose."

"You've got to realize there's a life outside of the furnace, son. You're thirty next month, so get out more. Have a date with a girl."

There was no time for Mrs. Truzynski's leaning shed that evening. He fixed the latch on her shed door, worked on the Studebaker awhile. Then the next day he decided to go back to Freda and Greta.

Their dimly lit living room went on and on. He sat freezing on a divan.

"A hand of Old Maid for you? Maybe a hand of Solitaire or Spite and Malice?"

"No," he said.

"He wants to hear our confession, Greta," Freda said. They looked at him. "Isn't it what you were thinking?"

He looked away, embarrassed.

"Absolve us," they said, "we've sinned."

They spoke in unison. They *shared* themselves—their frowns, the way they pursed their lips. They must have been surprised and amazed like this since birth: to see your sister, to look across the table and see, on the sad, startled face, your sister's mole at the center of your right cheek, your narrow lines of worry on her forehead.

Instead of absolving them of their sins, Mr. Truzynski got them talking. They looked away from each other, the two sisters, identical even to the plaid scarves, the shape of the eyes and nose, the curve of the lips, which were pale.

"We cried so hard, Mr. Truzynski."

"We screamed, Freda, when they tried separating us for any reason."

Their hands fidgeted. Their voices rose.

"We sleep in a double bed. In a double bed. We use the same soap. Our soap is the same. We both hold the frying pan when we make our supper."

Mr. Truzynski leaned forward, curious.

"We've had troubles. A boyfriend. No. No, *he* wasn't a boyfriend. Ken was a neighbor," Freda said.

"We liked him. We loved him. We'd chat with him," Greta said. "When he got married we were hurt. He wasn't a boyfriend. We tried to see him every day." Greta and Freda looked around now as if seeking Ken.

"We'd stare out the window. Ken Iverson. We'd run along up on the second floor, wait for him down on the street. We went to the place where he would have supper. Do you remember the Princess Cafe in East End? They said we were hounding him. We learned a lesson."

"Freda screamed at him one night, ran after him," said one sister.

"Uh-huh, Greta threw herself in front of his car."

"*You* did that!" Greta said.

"We did," they said. "Uh-hum, we were guilty of a breach of the peace. The court said we had to have a psychological and medical examination and said we should probably move to a hospital."

They looked at each other, saw the same face reflected in their eyes.

"We are two, Freda and Greta. The same woman. But there's no man for us," they said, "because we're identical."

"It must be lonely," said Mr. Truzynski. "Mother says I should get out to socialize more. I'm too serious for my own good, she tells me." He paused a moment. "Greta and Freda, sometimes you call me Mr.

Truth or Mr. Trust by mistake," the sergeant said. "I'm pretty trust-
worthy, it's true, in business and at home. You know I've had this business since a couple of years before I left for war. Never have a complaint
about my work. If you treat customers right, they appreciate it. They
know they can believe Tom Truzynski's truth. I'm trusted. I've been to
North and South Vietnam."

"Should we take him downstairs, Freda?"

"Where?" asked Mr. Truzynski.

"To see something. Just trust us."

Mr. Truzynski was beginning to like Freda and her sister. He actually put his hands on their shoulders.

They took him down the steep basement stairs to where it was
entirely black. Then they took him to another level where it was like
the beginning of the world in the white light of the flashlight. The
space around him; nothing was evident there, no pipes, nothing.
Wherever she shined the weak beam, nothing. The beam couldn't pen-
etrate to the ends of this level of the earth. The basement might have
gone right under the entire East End neighborhood, beneath St. Adalbert's Church, beneath *Szkoła Wojciecha* the Catholic school, beneath
the Parrot Tavern, the fire hall, the rest home. When no one spoke, Mr.
Truzynski thought how darkness covered the abyss of this basement in
the beginning, how the earth was waste and void like in this basement,
yet how the spirit of God was stirring in this basement.

Then Greta and Freda said, "God made the firmament." Their
voices startled Mr. Truzynski, who'd been thinking along the same
lines. He couldn't see either them or God. He shivered in the cold of
space without beginning. It was the cold, burnt-out blackness of
space in the basement, and he could smell tar. He wished he were in
uniform.

"Waters below the heavens were gathered into one place," Greta said.

"Then Greta, there was light in the firmament of heaven," said
Freda.

"The earth brought forth all kinds of creatures, Freda."

"Yes, sister," Freda said.

Tomasz Truzynski heard a rattling cough. "Where are you two ladies?" he called. Frightened, he said, "God, Lord, Jesus." He heard the sisters' dresses rustling.

"There's life, Freda," Greta said. Now they were moving somewhere, it sounded like to him, moving to find a truer combination of themselves.

When they flicked on a flashlight, to his amazement four hands held it. Where there'd been two women, now there stood one with four hands. Both stared out at Mr. Truzynski. Though he couldn't be certain in the light of that unsteady beam, it looked as though one sister rested her head upon the other's shoulder. And this one—was it Greta?—held her arms straight out under her sister Freda's arms; so four hands gripped the single light in the immense, cold night back in the beginning of time. Beneath the streets of East End, the sister with the head on her sister's shoulder thrust a leg between her sister's. Nestled like that, they stood in the act of creation—the double-in-one, the two-women-in-one beneath that neighborhood after Vietnam.

"Freda likes you," Greta said.

"Greta likes you," Freda said.

"Mr. Trust, try to fit your arms in here with ours," they said. "There's room for a head . . ."

By now he was on the floor. Frightened, he crawled into the darkness.

"We miss you, Mr. Truzynski. Only the Sister and the Holy Ghost." They snapped off the flashlight. "You crawled from our furnace, both furnaces. We felt you kick your way out. You wanted to be a priest. You were a son born of a furnace. Three, Mr. Truzynski, please help us and trust us that what we're doing is right."

Mr. Truzynski had seen men weeping, yelling strange words, imploring the Lord's salvation in Vietnam. Now he scrambled to where he thought the stairs were. The light found him.

"Three!" they said.

"Two!" Mr. Truzynski said.

"Three!"

"No, two," he said.

"No, three."

He kicked the table when he got home. Mother played Solitaire while Mr. Truzynski kicked the table. He took out his leather-covered Bible. He paged through it until he found it. " . . . the light shines in darkness," he read, "and the darkness grasped it not."

"Too much Old Maid?" she said. "Something from the icebox while I'm up? What did the three of you do tonight anyway, listen to Walter Cronkite?"

"Don't ever say three to me."

"Why?"

"Don't ask. That's all."

He went to bed to read. Now he could see why three was God's number. He found it right away—the depth of the riches of wisdom. "Of Him, and by Him, and in Him"—there it was, thought Mr. Truzynski. In any other way but the Blessed Trinity, three would be an unhealthy number.

The phone rang. Mother said for him to get it.

"Ken?" asked the voice.

The vapor- or fog-bearing air returned. After breakfast the next day he sat at the table drawing with a pencil and scratch paper. He made numbers one atop another. Mother shuffled cards for Solitaire. At ten o'clock he looked up.

"Do you have business calls to make?" Mother asked.

He told her he was going to hang around. He went out to the car, looked about the yard. Vietnam didn't mean much to others here at home, he thought, but in the jungle hills of the coast he'd seen what frightened men. He'd seen Commies coming at you so that the men he did know had turned and run. It was psychological.

All afternoon, as Mother played against herself at the table, Tomasz Truzynski thought about the one-in-three, the three-in-one, and of these two women and himself. He felt the strength of those figures, and the mystery and power of unity, of joining strength to strength—but not to two strengths. He thought what they created was sacrilegious. He'd witnessed something very odd in their basement.

"Yes, come over," they said when he called.

"It was so dark on the coast of Vietnam," he said as he sat in the living room. "Every night I'd look," he said, "but there was no light. Neither side. Freda and Greta, I'm telling you, all of us on both sides needed light. Instead it was noise. They had speakers. 'Americans,' the messages echoed through the hills. 'Lay down your arms. Turn against your comrades. Come with us.' That's all, night after night." Sergeant Truzynski paused a moment as if considering his words. "It sounded like the noise coming down through the vents of a furnace."

"Did you have someone to write home to?" they asked.

"Mother."

He asked them, "Don't you believe in love?"

Putting their heads together, they smiled. "Yes."

"In the negative properties of love?" he wanted to know.

Mr. Truzynski drove home later through the tar. Except for Ken, the twins hadn't known love either, he thought. He went to his room. He threw the pillow off his bed and, holding his breath, lay flat on his back until he couldn't breathe and felt himself turning blue.

For the first time, after supper, Sergeant Truzynski felt stronger than he'd been in a while, though. Something came to him in his room and during supper, and he went outside to dress in the shed. In the green uniform with the rifle and the ribbons, he drove in the Studebaker past St. Adalbert's, past the fire hall and Almo Hotel, to East End Drug. "Not three of them, the sisters and me, but two of us," he repeated.

"Did you reenlist, Tom?" Mr. Haugen, the drugstore proprietor, asked.

"Wrap up two bars of pretty, scented soap," Mr. Truzynski said.

He went past the creosote plant and didn't mind the tar this evening. Even Greta and Freda's tin-sided building looked appealing.

"Who's there?" they asked through the shade. "What does anybody want?"

"Ken Iverson," he said.

Two heads thrust out.

"It's Mr. Trust in uniform," Greta said.

"It's him," said Freda. "Not Ken at all."

He came in down the long hallway. "I have something for you," he said. He told them not to open the presents until tomorrow. "It's a test, a Civil Defense test."

The three of them sat in the kitchen. A wood cabinet painted with enamel paint ran along one whole wall. Against the other wall stood a sink and a mirror. Mr. Truzynski adjusted his barracks cap in the mirror. Of all the rooms he'd been in, the kitchen was the warmest. A sergeant of infantry happily sat sipping coffee from an old china cup, and across from him sat two sad sisters.

"It's good to be in uniform," he said.

"Do you take cinnamon on your toast?"

"Yes," he said.

The floor had been waxed. A little moonlight came in the window, resting on the waxed floor. He smiled, laughed, asked for more cinnamon.

* * *

The two fidgeted with each other all through the next day. Greta sprin-kled rosewater on her wrists. Freda patted her throat with powder. "*You* want to see Mr. Truzynski, don't you?" one would ask.

"*You* want to hear his voice."

Back and forth: "Fix your scarf! Fix your collar!" But Greta's scarf and Freda's collar went unfixed. Neither one listened. When one sister cupped her hands against the cold and her nerves, so did the other. When one looked in the foggy oval mirror to pat her hair or smooth her sweater, so did the other. But they didn't hear each other. They wanted to see him so they could open their presents.

He'd waited until very late in the afternoon to return. So far, he thought, they're happy with the pale green wrapping paper and the identical size of the soap boxes. Everything's identical. When they opened them, however (the soap was shaped like seashells), Greta and Freda looked at the other's present, then frowned. All his life, it seemed to Mr. Truzynski, it was as if he'd heard the world wailing down through the vents into his ears. Now more East End disappointment.

"I want that one," said Greta about the soap seashells.

She held up her present, but pointed to her sister's.

When Freda said, "Now I want that one *she* has," Mr. Truzynski had to cut the soap seashells in two, offering Freda a piece of pink to go with the green, Greta a piece of green to go with the pink. They held them up, a piece in each hand, so that they were identical. Then when Mr. Truzynski felt gratified he asked for toast and coffee.

Two days later they made him comfortable on the living room divan. In the cold, dark room he saw a register where warm air from the base-ment furnaces should have been rising. He looked down it. Except for at its very top where a little light from the ceiling penetrated, the tin shaft to the furnace was black, deep, cold. Wherever did it go besides the furnace, he wondered, to Vietnam?

He gave Greta a present this time. He brought only one present. "How beautiful . . . how heavenly," she said. Greta wound a shawl about herself and opened the wrapping when the sergeant left. It was Rose Petal Water. Seeing it, Freda and her jealous words started to come very fast and made no sense at all. She was saying, "We'll have to get some polish on the silverware . . . We'll have to paint the dishes, start the furnace . . ."

All Greta said was how tired and jealous Freda looked. Greta lay down on the divan, shawl around her shoulders. "You're looking so peaked and jealous," she said to her sister Freda.

In a few days Sergeant Truzynski knocked on the door. They peeked to see who it was. Then Freda's words, not Greta's, turned truthful. Freda was now overjoyed, for the sergeant gave only her a narrow, gift-wrapped box with a card. "The Patter," read the words on the present when she opened it. The device inside had a small handle. From it ran a metal section at the end of which was a round rubber piece about the size of a half-dollar. "The Patter Facial Aesthetics. A specially contrived instrument," the directions read, "for stimulating the facial muscles without irritating the skin. Is particularly beneficial in the reduction of double chin. Also restores contour to facial muscles by the only scientific method promoting the circulation. Pat a thin face gently, a plump face firmly."

As she patted away, Freda read over and over what the card said. It was a friendship card bought at East End Drug by an army sergeant:

> The only kind of card
> that's nice enough for you
> Is one that's filled
> with special thoughts
> and warmest wishes, too.

In the next weeks, only Greta received a present . . . then only Freda a present . . . then only Greta. The sergeant kept saying, "Not three, two." These days with Mother playing Solitaire, Sergeant Truzynski would draw on his scratch pad another number. And the women? If for forty-six years they'd been sad to see only themselves across the table, now things had changed and were very much better and worse.

In a building with quilted sides, they waited for a furnace cleaner. Something remarkable was happening. After their years together, they lived apart. One now ran through the vacant, high-ceilinged rooms upstairs crazily, happily, patting her face with "The Patter." The other twin spent her time in basements staring first into one furnace, then into another. She'd hear the other one above. From the attic to the basement, the one sister upstairs would whisper, sometimes even sing, to the one down below. Nothing could block out what the attic sister was saying. Funneled and shaped by tin, the word "I," traveling so many miles down through the house's vents and chutes, came out "Why?": "Why are you like this? Why are you breaking my heart?" Freda asked Greta.

"I don't know," Greta answered. It was like the war in Vietnam.

Then they'd go around the house wondering about a man's presents. "How can I be satisfied?" the sister who was left out each time would ask. "How can I be happy over your luck when *I'm* being neglected?" And all this time Sergeant Truzynski was drawing the number 1 on a scratch pad.

"My heart," jealous Greta would say to her sister.

"Yesterday, *my* heart," jealous Freda would say.

"Our hearts are splitting . . . they hurt us."

In the building of quilted sides, they never touched—or not often. On February afternoons when light returned to the northern latitudes where East End lay (to latitude 47° 10' N exactly) and when the sun peered under the shades and they could see prisms in the dust motes, then Greta would stand up and Freda sit down. Only occasionally would they see through the dust what had happened. Then they'd sit apart on the divan regretting their losses. Freda would stroke Greta's hair once again and Greta, Freda's; and they'd break into jealous sobs, and sometimes Sergeant Truzynski—who was stooping in the furnace below, who was actually crouching in the dark, central part of the house even a long time after the month that brought winter—sometimes Sergeant Truzynski sobbed for what was happening upstairs and wished to be back in the Heart and Flame to hear an ordinary man and wife crying.

His mother asked Tomasz what took up so much of his time these days.

"Freda . . . Greta."

"They've taken a liking, I guess, Tomasz."

"I suppose."

"Why not have them home for supper?"

"I will."

"Yes, you should."

What had been set in motion was not easy to stop. Here *or* in Asia.

"Here I am with my equipment," he'd say. He'd mix up the sisters. He'd come to see them not as two, as Greta and Freda, but as one. Sometimes confused, he combined the names into *Greda* instead of Greta, or *Freta* instead of Freda. After three more weeks Freda grew pale and weak from it all. If Freda was ailing, then Greta was ailing; but Greta didn't stop to help Freda who, toward the end of February, took to bed. Greta covered her with quilts which felt like tin. Greta brought milk, bread, and coffee to her sister. But Greta, no matter the attention, couldn't make Freda speak. "Freda, please speak to me," she'd beg. Nor could she restore Freda's feelings. From the bed Freda, or Freta, looked out at the pestilence and asked whether this was The Pesthouse she was suddenly inhabiting, then she'd turn her head away from the voice, the smile, the sister's red-lipstick mouth. Greta, the twin who wore rose-water and painted her face for Mr. Truzynski, slipped downstairs and was very, very happy and unhappy at the same time.

"Where's Freda?" When Sergeant Truzynski came by asking this, Greta said she didn't know about her sister, who lay with a broken heart beating up through her throat.

Alone upstairs, Freda spoke to herself. Freda responded to her own questions. "Are we staying in today?" she'd ask herself. "No, we're going out today," she'd answer herself. "Then what do you think of the weather?" she'd ask. "Oh, it's fine. Wait until you see it," she'd answer. How could she, Freda, get rid of forty-six years of Greta?

"Can I go up?" the sergeant would ask.

"No, I'm afraid to let you see her," Greta would say. "I'm afraid of her health. It may upset her. She's patting right now—facial aesthetics. Why not whisper through the vents?"

He'd kneel down by a register on the floor. "I . . . I," he'd begin to whisper. But before he could go on, the tin distance had shaped it to other words, or perhaps not words but numbers, and he would hear this patting sound that diminished each day so that finally it was just a "pat" or a "pat-pat" every seven or eight hours.

The mourners couldn't have numbered five the next week. They came, prayed and whispered over Freda (this was a whole week later, a whole week of whispered numbers), then they gave Greta a message concerning her loss. For Freda had died from the pain and loss of a veteran's love.

In her mother's wedding dress with the lace collar and cuffs lay dear Freda. Over the past few days Greta had reclaimed her half of their twin heart, but it had not been easy. All along she'd had to tell herself, "I'm so happy," knowing that half of her wasn't happy. Mr. Truzynski said what Freda in the coffin had was a badly bruised heart. Whispering to the dead Freda late at night, Mr. Truzynski, whom Greta had come to trust, would expect Freda to fidget with her cuffs, to cry out for love, to call for him through the vents as if she wasn't dead.

After sister Freda's burial in the dark in a snowstorm, only Greta kept Greta company in the big, lonely house. Now she had frequent, splitting headaches and worried about a stroke. He came over, sometimes between furnace calls. If she felt strong, she fixed his lunch or supper, but with twice as much work to do around the quilted building, she felt rundown all the time.

Of course the sergeant was sorry about Freda who'd died, but he also liked Greta. Something odd was going on with her. Her rosewater ran out and she no longer opened the powder, but she couldn't stop concentrating on what Sergeant Truzynski had meant by sending a drugstore card to her sister, especially one with such pretty words as "special thoughts" and "warmest wishes." They would sit and look at each other, the Vietnam war veteran who'd played such a part in the two hearts, and the remaining sister, who now very gently patted her forehead and cheek with her sister's "Patter." And finally the sergeant proposed marriage.

She'd say, "But whose passion were you talking about on that card to my sister? Whose? Whose?" for she repeated everything now as if to make up for Freda. She'd pat her face and ask, "The three of ours? *Our* passions?" (pat-pat)

"The two of yours," he'd say.

"Which one of ours particularly?" (pat)

"Why Freda's . . . Freda's," he'd say. "Or maybe yours. I just don't know."

Because of her sister's name (whispered softly by Mr. Truzynski twice up the vent), Greta's decline occurred deep down in the earth of the basement. That's all he had to do was whisper a name. "Freda, Fre-da," it had come upstairs—or was it saying "Freta?" she wondered. After hearing what she thought was Freda's name echoing all through the quilted house—in every room and closet—after that, Greta and the sergeant sat side by side in the first basement, the shallower basement; then later, weeks later, sat apart in separate corners at the same end of the quilted house's other, deeper basement. When her headaches worsened, Greta huddled at the opposite end. Across the void she'd call to him how God—"*God*, Mr. Truzynski, not Freda!"—had made the heavens and the earth. While all this time the sergeant, who in his mind had promoted himself to a much higher rank during the basement campaign, occupied another corner. There they crouched in opposite corners under the East End of Superior; and all they could see or hear of their future lives together down there, all these two could see or hear, was how the lighting of the furnace of light had brought whispers of regret.

A Concert of Minor Pieces

The cemetery was named after a church that had since been torn down. Most of the people who'd attended St. Adalbert's over the years were buried here. FRANEK PORZYCKI   ZOFIA KATZMARCK   TEOSIA MAREK   JOZEF KRYZANIAK read the names. In St. Adalbert's Cemetery, Leo Polaski now clipped grass from the edges of his family's graves. What else was there to do in retirement? Carved in the marble of his parents' gravestones was: ANTONI POLASKI, FATHER . . . AGATA, MOTHER . . . "WHAT THE HEART HAS OWNED AND HAD, IT NEVER LOSES."

At home Mr. Polaski's visitors, his cousin Chester and Chet's wife, late sleepers, would be having breakfast before packing the car for the trip home to Chicago. Instead of seeing them off, Leo Polaski wished he could linger in the cemetery where it was quiet. Here he was with loved ones. Sure Chet back at the house was his first cousin; but he was a stranger who'd changed his name, gotten married, and moved to Chicago, where he'd been a big number for forty years—owner of Orze Furnace and Sheet Metal. When in the old days Chet's kids visited Superior once in a while, they were like children of strangers. They had no interest in the area, kept saying they were bored, wanted to get back home where there were things to do at least. East End was drab. They, like their parents, wanted Chicagoland. Now, in case the cousin Chet wished to visit the family's graves (though he knew Chet wouldn't), Leo cleaned them very carefully. The weather was pretty good for this late in the year. Snow would come soon; but for a few hours now, it was clear, cold, and dry and the autumn woods empty of hunters. Below the cemetery flowed the Left-Handed River, heavy with the clay of the north. It was the clay his people were buried in.

As he pulled the last grass stems from the edge of the gravestone, something, the sun reflecting in a mirror, it looked like, caught his attention across the river. A breeze made the tops of the pines nod. The quiet morning. Then the sharp light as though someone were signaling him. Where the river swept around a bend lay a sedge meadow—rushes, cat-tails, alder brush. From where he stood to where the sedge meadow and valley ended and aspen and poplar grew, then pine—from here to the opposite hill—was a mile. It would be hard going in a swamp like that. He was thinking how he'd been down in there with Chet when they'd seen the Left-Handed the moment it awoke one year, the spring ice breakup. *We must've been twenty-eight back then, right before I was married,* he thought. Still one moment, in the next, the river had moved. Grating, heaving in places, spurting water up in others, layers of ice six, even eight feet high in a few places where the river's pressure had been great, began winding through the dry, spring land for as far up as the cousins could see. *A river will move in my lifetime,* Leo was thinking now when the reflection from across the meadow came again. Then a third time it came. Who could be down there? he wondered, thinking perhaps it was his eyes acting up. He'd been to the cemetery so often this fall that he could follow his own paths out through the withered grass.

* * *

"Good morning," Leo said in Polish as he came in. It was nearing eleven o'clock. "What a day. Too bad you leave. Your vacation's too short, you."

Up for an hour now, Helen Orze rubbed her hands with moisture cream. Chester adjusted his tie, lit a cigar, talked big city. "I've got something going back home," he said. "Some deals I've got."

"*Had!* Had big deals, Chester," Helen Orze said. "Get it through your head, you're retired." She warmed up coffee. "Remember what we brought for a present. You almost forgot."

"Oh, in the car," Chet said. Among his other great distinctions and accomplishments, he was an honorary choir member of St. Hyacinth Church off of North Milwaukee Avenue in a Polish neighborhood of Chicago. The choir was so good they'd recorded an album on whose cardboard jacket was Chet's name: "Cover financed by C. M. Orze." Chet was pleased. "See?" he said. "It's for you and Anna. Long-playing, recorded at St. Hyacinth."

Leo Polaski touched the tone arm to the record as Chet's wife Helen poured more coffee. Because the recording had been made live one Christmas at midnight Mass, you could hear sounds in the background—a kneeler scraping, a man coughing, the hushed stillness of the parish in the huge church, the magnificent organ. Mr. Polaski watched the needle, heard its slight scratch as he waited for *W Żłobie Lezy* and *Dzień Ten Nam Sam Pan Bóg Sprawił*. How funny . . . the movement of people, the coughing of people he'd never seen made them seem familiar. For sounds to echo like that, the church must have been very large, thought Mr. Polaski. Such old songs, too. Some they'd sung before the bishop closed their own neighborhood church. Some songs were a couple hundred years old.

"Here," Anna Polaski said, offering her husband a piece of thin, waferlike bread. Anna herself held a pink square of the wafer.

"Leo, aren't you going to share with us?" asked Chet.

"I'm sorry," said Leo Polaski. "I was thinking of my niece Stella. We should wait till next month for Christmas to break *opłatek* with each other."

"We won't be here then, hon," Helen said.

"We're retired," Chet Orze said, "but it don't mean we're not busy in Chicago with church matters."

Leo Polaski tried being upbeat and agreeable, but the phonograph record made him sad. He thought of St. Adalbert's Church and the school near the river—of their roofs, of their old brick walls. Overgrown fields now grew where the church stood. His niece Stanisława (Stella) had once held a recital in the St. Adalbert's School across from the church. She'd worn a white dress with a red sash, the colors of Poland, and spoken very plainly in the gymnasium. She'd said, "This is to be a concert of minor pieces. Mostly Chopin." How can it be so many years now? thought Mr. Polaski. Nothing is where it should be anymore. It's come down to remembering people in a graveyard. *Who had been signaling?*

"God, look, it's snowing," Chet said. "We gotta get going."

Shaking Leo's hand, he went out to warm the car up. "Here, Cousin Leo," Chet said when he returned, "break *opłatek* with me. I wish us happiness the rest of our days. I should've come to the cemetery."

He extended the small wafer-piece. Leo broke from it as he offered Chester his own *opłatek* wafer to break from. They ate what they'd taken from the other.

Chet Orze, a big man at St. Hyacinth's, was quiet after that. He took his and his wife's bags, hung the clothing bag in the backseat of the car, stored the suitcase and a smaller carryall bag in the trunk. The cold November air matched the dark gray skies, the weather having changed since morning.

"We'd better get going, hon," Helen said when she came out. Hugging Leo and Anna, she got into the car next to Chet. Arranging themselves for the trip, the Orzes waved and were off. After Chet left, Leo stood outdoors a few minutes longer.

Inside, he lifted the tone arm off of the phonograph record. What use in playing it? he thought. But as he looked for Chet's name on the record jacket, he changed his mind and lowered the phonograph needle to the start of the record. It seems like someone—the niece Stella, the neighbor Mr. Sleva—someone else should be here to share *opłatki,* he thought, as the organ began and the choir sang the Polish hymns.

He spent the afternoon listening to the record. Staring out at the dry, brown yard—a yard now being covered by snow—he played first one side, then the other. Then he played a Polonaise by Chopin. He remembered Chet's father and mother, Mr. Polaski's own uncle and aunt, as the Polonaise played. They were quiet, industrious people. He thought of Chet, remembered Chet helping Mr. Mylok repair the fence that kept mink in at the mink farm, remembered Chet a few years later, when he was starting out in sheet metal, asking him, Leo, to come to Chicago. How well Chester had taken care of him when he was there. Chet, who must've been very lonely back then, had tears in his eyes when he brought Leo back to the train station. *"Idź z Bogiem.* Good-bye. God be with you," Chet had said, hugging him. After that Chet had started the business going, gotten married. There wasn't much time for visiting his hometown and East End neighborhood anymore. Certainly not the cemetery.

At five o'clock Anna said, "We'll eat soon, Leo." By then snow covered the sidewalk, and he wondered about the Orzes.

Without listening to her, he put on his heavy coat and went out. Placing the remaining *opłatek* in his pocket, he cleaned the sidewalk. He was careful to sweep around where Chet and Helen walked on their way to the car. As long as he could see their footprints, they were still here with him; there were still Orziewiczes in East End.

"Leo," Anna called, "any mail today?"

"No," he said.

She watched him walking into the street. Streetlights were on. From the kitchen window, Anna Polaski could follow him. He was walking in the snow. Smoke from the Fredericka Flour Mill and dust from the fiberboard plant and coal dock blew and mixed with the snow. Mr. Polaski remembered Polish voices echoing in this neighborhood. What the heart has owned and had, it never loses, he thought. Even from Chet's church in Chicago echoes came, the echoes of old Polish songs . . . the singers' voices, *echa ojczyzny,* echoes of the Old Country.

Now Mr. Polaski thought of the old times as he walked again down Fourth Street toward the river and the cemetery where St. Adalbert Church used to stand. In winters past, the priest would have written in chalk "K.M.B.—Kaspar, Melchior, and Balthasar" over the church door. Mr. Polaski could remember the communion railing, the baptismal font. He remembered his great-aunt, a seamstress Mr. Polaski's father called by that name, *Krawiec.* For seventy years she'd bowed to her stitches. Years ago on windy, snowy evenings he'd have heard her singing at choir practice. Then Chet moved to Chicago with a new name, changed from Orziewicz, and Mr. Polaski's niece Stella had written that she was marrying a Swede from Minnesota. "What does it matter if I give up the piano, Uncle Leo?" she asked. "All I ever practice is the Polonaise."

The plaster statue of Adalbert, or *Wojciech,* the Patron Saint of Poland, had been sold from the courtyard. The votive candles, the veil and burse and some of the priest's vestments had been sold to a man in the country who had his own church; and the piano from the school gymnasium where Stella had played Paderewski and Chopin had been sold, and the folding wooden chairs and card tables, and the wooden floors and the bricks from the walls and from the foundation. Chet and Helen would be getting farther and farther away, he thought. Gone four hours and he missed them. Chicago was for big numbers like Chet Orze. Around here we are all minor players, minor pieces, Mr. Polaski thought. But not Chet. And not this Jacek Zukowski in the country with his own church and confessional out on County W.

He rubbed at the snow on the earth where St. Adalbert's had stood. In a few places snow melted on foundation stones that, placed in the ground a century before, were still here. Enough of the stones remained to show where at least part of a wall once was. Mr. Polaski also knew well where the altar sanctuary had been, the communion railing, the shrine to the Black Madonna of Częstochowa. The bishop had deconsecrated the ground when he'd directed St. Adalbert Church to be torn down.

Now someone Mr. Polaski could see only dimly walked past in the dark where Wojciech's statue once stood. Mr. Polaski looked into the snowy night. Where the St. Adalbert's altar had been, he knelt to pray against the devils that'd robbed him of Chester and of cousins in Buffalo and Cleveland, and of Krawiec, the seamstress, his great-aunt. Mr. Polaski whispered to St. Adalbert, their patron saint. In his pictures and on his statues, Wojciech, St. Adalbert, had a crown, fur robes, a staff. Through the snow Mr. Polaski could almost see him coming up from the river where Krawiec's voice was singing and where Stella played a nocturne. He thought of Victor Rutkowski, who'd operated a hoist at the lumber mill, of Adolph Wyzniewski, who'd given new Holy Name Society members a free haircut for half a century; some of the old neighborhood men . . . dead. He thought of Krawiec dead and in her grave, his great-aunt; and of his uncle, who'd fallen off the coal dock and drowned in Superior Bay. I never knew for a week what had happened to Uncle Stefan, he thought, and Chet was already Mr. Chester Orze, businessman, back then. *"Apostole i Męczenniku swięty, który opowiada jąc poganskiemu ludowi Prusakow . . . ,"* he thought he heard the dead people saying. He whispered a prayer to the Virgin. "Keep me from harm," he implored Her. He whispered a prayer to Poland and one to the priest, who'd been dead twenty years, and to the nuns, who were all gone, and to Stanisława Rozowska, his niece.

Leo's footprints were covered with snow as Wojciech, St. Adalbert, put out his hands. From as far away as Chicago, Mr. Polaski heard voices echoing prayer, echoes from the Old Country. "Awake," they said to him. Then Mr. Polaski prayed the way he used to and said he was grateful for his life. *"Boże! w obliczu którego żadna."* Then the ground was cold, and he saw everyone he'd ever known in the neighborhood—but from a distance. And it looked as though they were preparing to welcome him and in the forest where the light had come from he heard the wind and from far away voices saying a simple word, *"Bóg,"* that means "God" in Polish.

Alan Miller

ANTHONY BUKOSKI served as a Marine in DaNang, South Vietnam. He has been a car wash attendant, short order cook, camp counselor, and janitor. He has salvaged bauxite from derailed tank cars and worked in the complaint department at Sears. From these experiences, he drew material for his previous short-story collections, *Twelve Below Zero* and *Children of Strangers*. The latter, also published by Southern Methodist University Press, won the Oskar Halecki Prize from the Polish American Historical Association. Both books were presented Outstanding Achievement Awards by the Wisconsin Library Association. A three-time nominee for the Pushcart Prize, Bukoski teaches English at the University of Wisconsin–Superior and lives in the country outside of town. In 1997 he was featured in the PBS video *A Sense of Place: A Portrait of Three Midwestern Writers*.